"IT WAS AN ACCIDENT!"

"The trapdoor was left open, yes, but not to hurt you or anyone else. It was a stupid mistake, that's all."

Lydia nodded mechanically, knowing full well that the director was already thinking about trying to protect the theater's reputation.

Keenan, who had been standing at the back of the group, said, "If this was a made-for-TV-movie, people would think someone was trying to do away with Lydia."

He meant it as a joke, and everyone smiled or laughed. Everyone, that is, but Lydia.

"But the play's over," Lydia said. "Why would—"

"There's always the next show," Keenan pointed out. "If some jealous person didn't want you to get the lead in *Evita,* something like this would certainly stop you."

"Keenan, that's enough," Bill admonished. "Sometimes you go too far! No one would purposely hurt Lydia or any other member of the company."

Keenan shrugged. "Personally, I'd watch my step if I were you."

Dear Reader:

Just a moment of your time could earn you $1,000! We're working hard to bring you the best books, and to continue to do that we need your help. Simply turn to the back of this book, and let us know what you think by answering seven important questions.

Return the completed survey with your name and address filled in, and you will automatically be entered in a drawing to win $1,000, subject to the official rules.

Good luck!

Geoff Hannell
Publisher

STAGE FRIGHT

Look for all of Jahnna N. Malcolm's thrillers

Leo: Stage Fright
Virgo: Desperately Yours
*Libra: Into the Light**
*Scorpio: Death Grip**

from HarperPaperbacks

*coming soon

STAGE FRIGHT

by

Jahnna N. Malcolm

HarperPaperbacks
A Division of HarperCollinsPublishers

This is a work of fiction. The characters, incidents, and dialogues are products of the author's imagination and are not to be construed as real. Any resemblance to actual events or persons, living or dead, is entirely coincidental.

HarperPaperbacks   *A Division of* HarperCollins*Publishers*
10 East 53rd Street, New York, N.Y. 10022

Copyright © 1995 by Malcolm Hillgartner and
Jahnna Beecham
All rights reserved. No part of this book may be used or reproduced in any manner whatsoever without written permission of the publisher, except in the case of brief quotations embodied in critical articles and reviews. For information address HarperCollins*Publishers*,
10 East 53rd Street, New York, N.Y. 10022

Cover illustration by Danilo Ducak

First HarperPaperbacks printing: July 1995

Printed in the United States of America

HarperPaperbacks and colophon are trademarks of
HarperCollins*Publishers*

❖ 10 9 8 7 6 5 4 3 2 1

For Larry Bograd and Coleen Hubbard

chapter 1

The lights went down for the final time, and the crowd burst into applause.

Exiting to the wings of the Dallas Youth Theater, Lydia Crenshaw knew her horoscope had been wrong. That morning she'd grabbed the newspaper from her brother, Jake, to see what the closing night of *My One and Only* held in store.

LEO—*You, who love the spotlight so much, should stay away from it today. You could get burned. Think about events taking place in your life. Something isn't quite right, but don't jump to conclusions. Think, Leo, before you roar!*

Stay away from the spotlight! Lydia chuckled as

she listened to the outpouring of support and adulation from her audience. Never!

The closing night of any show was always bittersweet for Lydia. Bitter because something magical was ending. Something that a few weeks earlier seemed like it would never come together. Sweet because there was nothing better than an auditorium full of people watching her every gesture.

Rehearsing and performing a musical was like riding a speeding roller coaster. A lot of high thrills and slow lows, and in-between some very dangerous and scary curves.

This production had been particularly demanding since Lydia was playing the lead role of Edith. And rehearsal time with her leading man and former boyfriend, Keenan, had been limited because he'd started doing TV commercials, which swelled his already big head.

"Places for the curtain call," Lydia heard her friend Anna Jo Gender whisper into a headset.

Anna Jo—known as A. J. to one and all—was the production's stage manager. It was her job to make sure everyone offstage was where they should be and that everything onstage happened exactly on cue. A tough job, but A. J., already a

veteran of many productions, made it look easy—
even if she ate too much junk food in the process.

Lydia moved to A. J. and patted her on the
back. "Thanks for a great run," she whispered. "I
hate it when a play ends. Especially when it's one
I've loved as much as this."

"A few more minutes and it'll all be over," A. J.
said in her matter-of-fact Southern drawl. "Then
it'll be time to start rehearsals for the next show."

Lydia couldn't help but chuckle. A. J. was so
even-keeled. Lydia was the complete opposite.
The queen of emotions. That's what made them
such good friends. They balanced each other out.

"Okay, everybody, places for the curtain call,"
A. J. repeated into the headset. "Places!"

Lydia waited, along with the other leads,
while the chorus members and bit players took
their places on stage.

Being the star, she would come on last, take
Keenan's hand, and if past nights were any indica-
tion, receive a standing ovation when she took
her bow.

To some people, what Lydia had achieved by
her midteens was an amazing success story—but
not to Lydia. She'd loved to perform for as long as
she could remember. If you believed her mother,

Lydia's very first sentence was, "Mommy, watch me!"

As a preschooler, there were dance lessons. In first grade, she began taking ballet at the Dallas Academy. The next year, she started studying piano and voice. By fourth grade, tap dancing and acting were added to the weekly list of places to be after school. It seemed that Lydia's mother was always dropping her off someplace, then rushing home to sew a new costume.

Not that Lydia minded. She *loved* to perform. When her parents entertained—before their divorce one year before—Lydia was always called upon to dance and sing.

"It's your destiny to be a great star," her mother had said, "because you're a Leo."

Maybe it's true, Lydia thought as she waited for her curtain call. *A lot of famous actors are Leos.* Lucille Ball of the classic *I Love Lucy* TV series. Whitney Houston, Madonna, Patrick Swayze, and Christian Slater—all Leos! In fact, Lydia heard that more actors were Leo than any other sign, so Lydia was in very good company.

"Lydia, standby," A. J. whispered to her.

The curtain and stage lights went up, and the applause increased as the supporting cast took its bow. Lydia stepped in between the darkened folds of the curtains.

Keenan Taylor, who played Billy Chandler, the leading man in the show, was directly across from her in the opposite wing.

She met his eyes and felt as if a dark cloud suddenly passed over her.

"If it hadn't been for you," she murmured, staring directly at the tall blond teen, "everything would have been perfect." Theirs had been an intense relationship from the moment they'd met. That was during auditions for *The Music Man* two years before.

They started dating and were instantly serious. Lydia had strongly considered going to the same college drama program with Keenan.

Then Keenan got a talent agent and his good looks and success in local television commercials went directly to his head. He started cheating on Lydia and that was it. They split, shaking the high-school theater community. The breakup hadn't been easy. There were big shouting matches, lots of door slamming. And tears. Lydia's tears.

As she stared at the tall blond boy, so handsome in his dapper twenties suit, it was easy to see how someone would fall for him. But once she had gotten to know him and discovered he was a walking ego ready to sell his soul for a television commercial, Lydia couldn't figure out why she'd stayed with him.

"A big waste of time," she said, forcing a smile in his direction. He'd caught her staring and had waved.

I guess I should let bygones be bygones. She waved back. *After all, the show is a hit and in just a moment it will be over.*

But it was hard for Lydia to forget the hours they'd spent fighting in rehearsal. Time and again Bill Glover, their director, would take Keenan's side. Of course that was understandable. Bill had wanted his daughter, Elizabeth, to play the female lead in *My One and Only*. Elizabeth, who couldn't sing or dance but was the apple of her father's eye. Lucky for Lydia, the producer of the Dallas Youth Theater squashed that idea. Unfortunately, Bill never completely got over it.

But that was history now. Lydia, Keenan, and Bill put their differences aside, the cast pulled together, and the show had become an obvious hit.

"I wish we could go on doing this show forever,"

Lydia whispered to A. J., who had taken off her headset and come to stand beside her in the wings.

"Speak for yourself," A. J. said, watching the supporting cast finish its bows. "You're not the one who has to make tea and those little cakes every night. You're not responsible for seeing that the props are returned to the right prop table. That the costumes are clean and ready. That the stagehands don't forget to reset the stage during intermission. That Keenan has his favorite brand of bottled water so he doesn't throw a fit. One thing I will miss, though, is seeing you play Edith."

"It's my favorite role ever," Lydia replied.

"Until *Evita,*" A. J. said with a grin.

Evita was the next scheduled show. And the lead role was one of the plums in musical theater.

"A lot of people will be trying out," Lydia reminded A. J.

"Oh, you know you'll get it!" A. J. said, not buying Lydia's false modesty. "You're the best actress in this whole company. There's no one who can touch you."

In the dark, Lydia smiled. She wouldn't say so out loud, but she agreed. Why shouldn't she get the part of Evita? She was the best, and show after show proved it. Besides, her whole life was dedicated to the theater. The place she felt most alive was on the stage.

"Okay, Lydia," A. J. said, pointing to Keenan, who was now taking his bow. "It's your turn."

The young women embraced. "See you at the party," Lydia said, not moving.

"Lydia?" A. J. said, gestured toward Keenan, who was now standing with one hand pointing toward the wings.

"Always make 'em wait," Lydia told her friend. Then, with an upward tilt of her chin, she strode onto the stage. The audience instantly leaped to their feet.

"Bravo! Bravo!"

Lydia flashed her winning smile.

Yes. This is where I belong!

chapter 2

"Miss Lydia, you were absolutely *fab*-ulous!" Robin McCready called out from the wings the moment the curtain closed for the last time. The tall, lanky redhead ran on and, lifting Lydia off her feet, twirled her around. "Please, take me to Hollywood with you!"

"Did you really like it, Rob?" Lydia asked, laughing at her friend's exuberance.

"Speaking only as this show's designer," Robin said, setting her down and looking straight into her eyes, "as well as your biggest fan and most honest friend, I am telling you now that tonight you were brilliant!" He turned to the other cast members, still milling around on the stage exchanging hugs. "She was brilliant!"

"Robin, Lydia, settle down," a male voice boomed from the wings.

"Oh, no!" Rob whispered in mock horror. "We're in trouble with the great and powerful Garrett Hughes."

Lydia nodded, rolling her eyes. Although he was their classmate, Garrett acted more like a boring middle-aged man than a seventeen-year-old. As the Youth Theater's technical director, he took his job *very* seriously.

"My crew is waiting to strike the set," Garrett continued. "And unless you two vacate the stage, we'll be here working all night."

Robin and Lydia looked at each other and back at Garrett. "Well, ex-*cuse* me!" they shouted in unison.

"What are you wearing to the party?" Robin asked as he ushered Lydia from the stage toward the dressing rooms. "Something scandalous, I hope? Maybe that daring swimsuit costume from the show, with a pair of red spiky heels?"

"I just threw something together," she replied, trying to sound casual. "I hope you like it."

She'd only spent two weeks scouring the department stores to find just the right outfit for the party. *With practically zero budget, it's tough.*

"Well, don't hang out in front of your mirror too long," he said, moving off. "I'm going on ahead to make sure the CDs will make people get up and dance!"

Lydia retired to the girls' dressing room to remove her stage makeup and hang up her costume for the wardrobe people to collect. When she finally reached for her party clothes, she saw that her hands were shaking. She shook them hard. *Will you relax? It's only a party.*

But the party *was* important. Lydia knew that what she wore and how people treated her were almost as important as the play. *If you want to stay a leading lady, you have to act like one.*

While the other girls hurried out of the dressing room, anxious to join the party, Lydia took a deep calming breath and got dressed.

First, the ultrashort leather skirt she'd found at a closeout sale at Neiman-Marcus. Next the high heels—tough to walk in, but they made her legs look terrific. Then the sheer silk blouse, which had cost a fortune but was worth it.

"Lydia? You coming?" A. J. shouted through the dressing-room door. "The party's started."

"In a minute." Lydia took her place in front of

her mirror and oh, so carefully applied her lipstick. *Make 'em wait. Always.*

She'd had to wear her short, auburn hair flat like a twenties flapper for the play. Now she sprayed it with a style set and spiked it dramatically. The long red chiffon scarf was the finishing touch to add just the right flair.

Lydia studied her reflection and then carefully blotted her lips in a perfect kiss on her mirror. *Right. Here goes!*

She took the shortest way to the green room, the backstage lounge where the actors waited their turn to go on stage. Usually it was a dingy mess, but tonight it had been transformed with crepe-paper streamers and strobe lights into the party room.

Lydia walked directly across the stage, being careful to avoid the trapdoor in the center of the floor. It had been used once during the show. The rest of the time it was kept locked. Still, Lydia never trusted it and always, always walked around it.

The noise of pounding hammers and whirring power screwdrivers was deafening as Garrett's crew dismantled the set. Lydia stopped for a moment, and covered her ears. Seeing the stage being returned to its usual bareness, she sadly realized this show was really, really over.

"What are you doing?" Garrett asked, coming up behind her.

"Just looking," Lydia said. "Is that a problem?"

"You turn your costumes back to wardrobe?" he asked, not answering her question.

"They're in my dressing room," she told him. "I thought wardrobe would collect them."

"We're not your slaves, Miss Lydia," he snapped. "After we're done here, go back to the dressing room and carry your costumes to wardrobe."

"Yes, sir!" Lydia clicked her heels together. "If it'll make you happy, I can go get them right now." She turned back toward the dressing room, but Garrett grabbed her arm with just enough force to stop her.

"I said, *after* we're done," he said. "Now get out of here before you get hurt."

What a jerk! Lydia crossed into the far wing toward the green room, where, from the sounds of it, the party was in full swing. Just as she reached the door she sensed some movement in the dark hall to her right.

"Keenan, that tickles my neck," a giggling voice said from the darkness.

"It's meant to," Keenan responded, making little kiss sounds.

Lydia was instantly repulsed. She put one hand on her hip and said, "Cars have backseats for that sort of thing. Why don't you two go find one your size?"

Keenan broke away from the girl he was kissing and stepped into the light. "Lydia? I didn't see you there."

"Would it have mattered?" she asked in her steeliest voice.

He matched her tone. "No, I guess it really wouldn't." Then he pulled a petite blonde into the light, circling her waist with his hand. "Have you met Jill?"

"We've only worked together every day for the past month," Lydia said sarcastically. The girl had played one of the lead dancers in the musical. Only a sophomore at school, Jill had done a good job (though Lydia wasn't about to admit that now).

Lydia forced an icy grin at the young girl. "Way to score, Jill."

"Ah, thanks," Jill replied, not really sure what Lydia was referring to.

"*Ciao!*" Lydia turned, hoping they didn't notice her reddened cheeks. It was bad enough knowing Keenan had gotten a new girlfriend. But to catch them in the act . . . *major humiliation*.

The party was in full swing when Lydia flung open the door. She hesitated for just the right amount of time in the doorway, throwing her long red scarf dramatically across her shoulder.

As she'd hoped, the party activity came to a sudden halt. Applause exploded from around the room.

Robin McCready, long acquainted with Lydia's methods, crooned, "There she is, Miss Youth Theater. There she is, our big star!" He sidled up to her like an emcee at a beauty pageant. "With her long red scarf, her beautiful legs, and her enormous ego . . ." This last part cracked everyone up.

Lydia pretended to strangle him with the scarf, to gales of approving laughter.

"Help! A. J., save me!" Robin dropped to his knees, grabbing A. J. by the back of her black tuxedo jacket. The stage manager was standing at the hors d'oeuvre table, clutching a plate piled high with chips, a sandwich, and a thick slice of chocolate cake.

"Here." A. J. stuffed a chocolate-chip cookie into Robin's mouth. "Eat this. It'll make you feel better."

Lydia shook her head. A. J. was a typical techie. She'd go for two days without food, then gorge herself with junk. No wonder she struggled with her weight.

Lydia scanned the room while Robin hurried to change the music. Keenan and Jill had also entered the party and were now wrapped in each other's arms in the corner. *How cozy.*

Trish McClelland, who'd played Mickey, Lydia's sidekick in the show, and a stagehand named Roger Travis were huddled on the old faded pink couch in the corner.

Another couple. *Wonderful.*

Lydia was starting to feel more than a little left out when she spotted an extremely good-looking boy standing by himself, leaning against the far wall. As his eyes met hers one corner of his mouth curved up in a tantalizing hint of a smile.

It took Lydia a moment to place him, as she hadn't seen him at the theater before. Then she realized that he was the same handsome boy she'd seen in the halls at her high school, the John Connally High School for the Performing Arts. Without thinking, her lips formed his name. "Eric."

Before she could say a word to this handsome

boy, the affected accent of her director pierced the air.

"Lydia, darling, you gave the performance of your life!" Bill Glover crossed the dance floor toward her, with arms wide open. "I was simply thrilled and amazed at what you did tonight."

"You were?" Lydia hoped he was being sincere. As good as she felt about the audience's response, it was nice to know that her director thought she'd done well. Particularly since he was to direct the next show, too.

"But of course!" he said, folding her into his arms. "Everything you've done on this stage before was trite and amateurish compared to your portrayal of Edith tonight."

It was classic Bill Glover—to compliment Lydia at the same time as he knocked her down.

Before releasing her from his hug, the director whispered in her ear, "Check your dressing room before you leave. I left a little something as a token of my appreciation for all your hard work."

"What did our great dictator—I mean, director—want?" Robin asked, joining her.

Lydia shrugged. "He said he left something for me in my dressing room. Probably just a card, if I know him."

Robin folded his arms and pouted. "He probably left flowers, trying to overshadow my gift."

"You left me a gift?" Lydia was touched. "Oh, Rob, that's sweet."

Robin dropped his usual flamboyant facade. "I signed it 'your secret admirer.' I hope you don't mind."

Secret admirer. Lydia couldn't help it, but hearing those words made her eyes turn instantly to Eric. He was still standing against the wall, sipping a soda. If he was striking a pose on purpose, it was one that caught Lydia's eye. Dressed in black jeans, Doc Marten's, and a black shirt with a banded collar, he radiated a brooding mystery that was very attractive.

"Earth to Lydia!" Robin waved his hand in front of her face. "Hello? Anyone in there?"

"What!" Lydia stepped back, blinking in surprise. "What's the matter?"

"Here I'm trying to be sincere and you don't even notice." Robin pressed his wrist to his forehead dramatically. "Crushed. I'm totally crushed."

"I'm sorry, Rob." Lydia felt her cheeks heating up. "It's just that I'm, um, overwhelmed."

Rob cocked his head and studied her face carefully. "Really?"

Luckily, someone had put on a CD of old movie tunes and the opening phrases of the Fred Astaire and Ginger Rogers classic "Let's Face the Music and Dance" filled the room. Changing the subject in the most dramatic way possible, Lydia leaped into Robin's arms in a parody of glamorous ballroom dancing.

He was surprised, but happy. As they twirled around to the delight of the onlookers, Lydia kept an eye peeled to see if Eric was watching her, too. He was—but not with the same pleasure as everyone else. His expression seemed to say, "Major show-off."

Hmm. He's tougher than I thought.

She and Robin ended their routine and took some bows. Then Keenan took control of the music and put on a contemporary ballad. Lydia let herself drift away from Robin into the crowd, hoping that Eric would seize the chance to come over and get acquainted. But A. J. intercepted her.

"There's someone I want you to meet," A. J. said.

"What's his name?" Lydia asked.

"*His?* Lydia, you're so conceited," A. J. said with a smile. She pointed to a girl standing awkwardly in the corner.

The girl was dressed in a very old-fashioned style—1950s cotton party dress with anklets and mary janes. Her dishwater-blond hair was pulled into a ponytail at the base of her neck and tied with a pastel bow. She was the type who'd never be noticed, unless one ran her over.

"Isn't that the girl from Wallflowers Anonymous?" Lydia asked breezily.

A. J. slapped her wrist. "Be nice."

They worked their way over to the new girl, who, upon seeing them, straightened her skirt and forced a shy smile.

"Lydia, say hello to Paige Adams," A. J. said. "I kept running into Paige around the theater. Turns out she's your biggest fan."

"Really?" Lydia gave Paige a dazzling smile.

"I came to every performance of *My One and Only*—just because of you," Paige murmured. Her voice was soft, almost trembling with awe. "I could watch you forever!"

"Why, that's so nice," Lydia replied. She was genuinely flattered.

"I know this is silly," Paige continued. "But I left a little present for you in your dressing room. I asked A. J. and she said you wouldn't mind."

"A present?" Lydia repeated, glancing at A. J., who nodded.

"It's a pin that belonged to my grandmother," Paige explained. "She gave it to me before she died."

"Oh, I couldn't take something like that—" Lydia began.

"Please." Paige touched her lightly on the arm. "I want you to have it."

"Well . . . thank you," Lydia said graciously. "How is it that you came to every performance?"

"I'm new in town," Paige said, without looking up. "I don't know many people, don't have any friends. But I've always loved the theater. And I found out that the bus near my house stops right near the Youth Theater. So I came to opening night, just on a whim. And I've seen every show since."

"Are you in theater, too?" Lydia asked.

"Oh, not like you," Paige replied. "I did a little acting in my hometown. But nothing serious. Mostly children's shows. One time I played Glinda the Good Witch, in *The Wizard of Oz*. It was a pretty good production, until the boy playing the Scarecrow came down with a strep throat and . . ."

Boring. Lydia felt her mind wander as Paige listed off her modest accomplishments. After all, why should she endure the ramblings of a little theater groupie when dark, mysterious Eric was somewhere nearby?

"Look, Paige, I'd love to chat," Lydia said bluntly, "but I promised my friends I'd—"

"Oh, you don't have to explain," Paige said, quickly retreating toward the door. The crestfallen look on the girl's face made Lydia almost wince with guilt.

"Why don't you come to the next meeting of the Youth Theater's drama club?" Lydia said impulsively. "We're called Caught in the Act and we meet every Wednesday night."

"I—I don't know," Paige stammered. "If I'd fit in, I mean."

"Of course you would," Lydia said, dismissing the girl's worries with a wave of her hand. "Look, we just get together to talk theater, work on our audition pieces for future shows—"

"You mean, you have to perform?" Paige gasped.

"Only if you want to. And we plan group trips to see the Broadway touring shows when they come through Dallas and Houston. Or do fundraisers for the Youth Theater—stuff like that."

"If you think no one would mind . . ."

"Absolutely not. Try to make it," Lydia said.

"Okay, then. I'll be there!" Paige was thrilled. The gratitude shining in her eyes made Lydia feel pleasantly warm inside.

As Lydia and A. J. walked away A. J. hissed, "I just wanted you to say hello. You didn't have to ask her to join our club. We don't even know her."

"It's the least I could do," Lydia shot back. "The poor kid's new and doesn't know a—"

"Excuse me?" It was Paige again, tugging gently at Lydia's sleeve. "I'm sorry but you didn't say where the club meets."

"Oh. At the Backstage Club."

"It's a coffeehouse two blocks from the theater," A. J. explained. "You can't miss it."

Paige thanked them and melted back into the crowd.

"Tell the truth," Lydia teased A. J. "It feels good to do something genuinely nice for someone every now and then, doesn't it?"

A. J. shrugged. "Looks like you've got a loyal fan for life."

Lydia smiled coyly. "Icing on the cake, that's all."

She didn't mention that she would have said almost anything to get away from Paige, just so she could talk to Eric.

A. J. went to get a glass of punch, and Lydia seized the moment to introduce herself to Eric.

She had barely said hello when he asked, "Listen, a bunch of us are going out for a late supper. Would you care to join us?"

Lydia blinked in surprise. *Wow. He gets right to the point.* "Um, sure." Too eager. Take it slow. "Well, maybe. Let me check with my friend A. J. She's my ride—but she'll probably say yes."

"Great," he said. "Let's meet in the parking lot and we'll decide where to go."

Perfect. Lydia suddenly felt like soda pop inside. All bubbly and fizzy. She couldn't wait to tell A. J. about the change in plans.

"Eric asked you to go out?" A. J. asked, a deep frown on her face.

Lydia recognized that look. A. J. was feeling left out again. *Quick, better fix this.*

"Well, no, not on a date," Lydia stammered. "A bunch of people are going out for a bite, and he invited us along."

"Us?" A. J.'s frown disappeared. "Eric wanted *me* to go, too?"

"Well, of course. He specifically asked me to ask you." Lydia figured that a little white lie wouldn't hurt. Especially if it made A. J. feel better.

"Eric asked you to ask me?" The frown was turning into a smile. "Well, all right, then!"

"Come on." Lydia tugged on her friend's arm.

"Wait a minute." A. J. dug in her heels. "Don't you need your purse?"

"My purse?"

"In your dressing room." A. J. talked to Lydia as if she were a small child.

"Oh, right," Lydia said. "I'll be right back. Make sure no one leaves without me!"

Lydia decided to skip the hall and cross the stage to get to the dressing room. It was the fastest way, and Garrett and his techies had long since cleared out.

The stage was in near-total darkness as she stepped into the wings. *That's odd,* Lydia thought. *The techies forgot to leave the ghost light on.*

She crept along the wall, searching in the dark for the switch that turned on the work lights. But when she flicked the switch, nothing happened.

Maybe a fuse is out. Lydia inched forward into the darkness. She decided one of the technicians must have been fiddling with the light board and damaged it. *Garrett will have his hide, for sure!*

Lydia passed through the slit in the heavy velvet curtains onto the stage. She knew its configuration by heart, having worked on it so much. A few steps more and she'd be across. Just a quick stop in the dressing room, and then a run back to meet Eric.

Maybe Keenan would see her with Eric. *Perfect.*

As Lydia reached center stage, her mood was upbeat, her thoughts running wild with romance and intrigue.

Five more steps and I should be there. One, two—

She stepped forward into nothingness. First her foot. Then her body. And then she was falling. . . .

Lydia screamed, a bloodcurdling yell that echoed madly around the vast, empty theater.

chapter 3

"Lydia? Lydia, can you hear me?"

Side aches. Leg hurts. Neck's sore. Her eyes still closed, Lydia slowly took inventory of the pains racking her body.

"Are you okay?"

That voice. Unfamiliar.

Lydia felt something—a hand, strong and warm—brush against her face. Struggling, she opened her eyes.

Eric's face. Close enough to feel his warm breath on her cheek. His dark eyes were clouded with concern.

"Are you hurt?" he murmured. "You took a major tumble, Lydia. Does anything feel broken?"

It was then that Lydia was forced to remember that this wasn't a dream. That she had a body that had suffered more than a few cuts and bruises.

"I don't think so," she managed to say.

"You're lucky I heard you scream," Eric said, taking her hand. "Or you might've fallen and really hurt yourself!"

"But I did fall," Lydia murmured, trying to rise up on one elbow. The second she did, pain shot up her arm. "Yeow."

"Easy now," he said. "You're right. You did fall. But somehow your scarf snagged a plank on the stage floor, or you would've dropped all the way to the concrete below. "Come to think of it," he added, loosening the scarf from around her neck, "you're lucky you didn't strangle yourself."

"What happened?" Lydia's arm ached and she was confused.

"All I know is there was enough light coming from the green room for me to see you holding on for dear life," Eric explained. "I guess instinct took over, because the next thing I remember is grabbing you and pulling you to safety."

"My hero," Lydia tried to say, but her lips felt parched. She wished she could have some water.

"Give her some air," Bill Glover ordered as he arrived on the scene. "Come on, folks, make way."

Folks? Lydia squinted at her surroundings. She was on a couch stored in the prop room, which was one of several storerooms located beneath the stage. Eric was still kneeling beside her, but now a crowd had gathered in the dim light around him.

"How'd I get in the prop room?" she managed to whisper.

"Eric carried you over from the pit." This voice belonged to A. J., who knelt down beside Lydia.

"What happened exactly?" Bill Glover asked, rubbing his neck like he always did when he was nervous.

"I was heading toward the dressing room," Lydia said slowly. "The work lights on stage were off, for some reason—even the ghost light. Next thing I knew I was dropping through space. I guess my scarf caught on something and broke my fall."

"Good thing, too," Robin said, bringing her a cup of water, "or you might have broken your back!"

"Don't drink that," A. J. warned, "until the paramedics arrive and check you out."

"Paramedics?" Lydia frowned. "I think I'm okay. Sore, but nothing feels broken."

"What I want to know," Bill declared to everyone present, "is who's the idiot who left the trapdoor open!"

No one came forward with the answer.

"Trapdoor?" Lydia sat up with Eric and Robin's help. "I fell through the trapdoor?"

The glum faces surrounding her nodded.

"We were partying in the green room," A. J. said, "when we heard this horrible scream coming from the stage. We rushed in. It was dark. I went straight to the work-lights switch, but couldn't get it to work."

"I couldn't get them to work, either," Lydia cut in.

"Eric called for help," A. J. continued. "Someone must've gone to the booth and turned on the lights—"

"I did," Garrett Hughes said, stepping forward. "I was up there, ah, reprogramming the board when I heard the scream."

"When I saw that trapdoor gaping open, and Eric struggling to free you, I feared the worst," A. J. said.

"You mean, you feared that I was okay," Lydia joked, wincing a little as she chuckled.

That Lydia was able to make light of the situation

seemed to allow everyone to breathe a deep sigh of relief.

"So you're all right?" Bill Glover asked, genuinely concerned.

"A little bruised and sore," Lydia said, taking a sip of water. "But I think I'm okay."

"You could have been seriously hurt," Robin muttered as he took the glass from Lydia. "I mean, you could have died because of someone's carelessness." For once he was not joking.

"It was an accident," Bill Glover said quickly. "The trapdoor was left open, yes, but not to hurt you or anyone else. It was a stupid mistake, that's all."

Lydia nodded mechanically, knowing full well that the director was already thinking about trying to protect the theater's reputation.

Keenan, who had been standing at the back of the group, said, "If this was a made-for-TV movie, people would think someone was trying to do away with Lydia."

He meant it as a joke, and everyone smiled or laughed. Everyone, that is, but Lydia.

"But the play's over," Lydia said. "Why would—"

"There's always the next show," Keenan

pointed out. "If someone didn't want you to get the lead in *Evita*, something like this would certainly stop you."

"Keenan, that's enough," Bill admonished. "Sometimes you go too far. No one would purposely hurt Lydia or any other member of the company."

Keenan shrugged. "Personally, I'd watch my step if I were you." He raised an eyebrow.

As Lydia watched him loop his arm around Jill and exit the prop room, she shivered involuntarily. *Was that some kind of threat?* She certainly took it that way.

Moments later the paramedics arrived. Even though Lydia said she felt fine, they checked her over carefully before releasing her to go home.

Lydia realized she must have banged her left ankle on the edge of the stage because it hurt to walk. Eric caught hold of her arm and held open the door of the theater. The flowery aroma of the Texas spring washed over her as they stepped out into the night air.

"Seems like we'll have to wait for another night for our dinner," Eric said as they waited for A. J. to bring her car around.

"Yeah, I feel a little wobbly tonight," Lydia

admitted. "I just want to go home and sit quietly."

And shake! It was taking every ounce of her willpower not to have a nervous collapse. She'd stared death in the face and it was truly frightening.

A. J. pulled her old orange Toyota up to the front steps of the theater. Eric opened the passenger door for Lydia and instructed A. J, "Take her right home and put her to bed."

A. J. nodded. "Sure thing."

Eric shut the door, then crossed around to the driver's side. "Thanks for inviting me tonight," he told A. J. "I can safely say this is the most excitement I've had since I moved to Dallas two years ago."

A. J. blushed. "Didn't I tell you showbiz was exciting?"

"You were right." Eric rapped his knuckles on the top of the car. "Catch you two later."

A. J., being a little overexcited, put her foot to the pedal and her tiny car shot out of the parking lot.

Lydia's mouth hung open in stunned surprise. "A. J.? *You* invited Eric to the play?"

A. J. bobbed her head up and down so hard her short dark hair flopped in her face. "He's cute, isn't he? No. Cute's not the word. Handsome. Mega-handsome. Cover-guy handsome. And nice. Soooo nice."

Lydia couldn't believe it. Her normally sarcastic friend was acting like a giggly fifth-grader. "A. J., you realize you are raving, don't you?"

"I can't help it." A. J. took both hands off the wheel and shrugged. "He's just so wonderful."

Lydia leaned back against the headrest and sighed. "*Wonderful* is the understatement of the year."

A. J. hadn't heard her. She was too wrapped up in her own thoughts. "And not affected, like Keenan or all of those other guys at our school. I mean, he must *know* he's handsome, but it doesn't affect the way he relates to people. He seems to accept them for what they are."

Lydia smiled, thinking about his dark eyes with their little gold flecks. "He's a poet, right?"

"He writes pretty well, but his first love is art," A. J. informed her. "He says he wants to try his hand at set design."

"Really? So you're friends?"

"We've had a few classes together," A. J. said. "Besides being unbelievably good-looking, he's really intelligent and talented."

"*Everyone* at Connally High is talented," Lydia said, "otherwise they couldn't have gotten into a school for the arts."

"No, but I mean he's really, *really* good," A. J. insisted. "Not only at writing and art, but in science and math, too."

Lydia grinned. "He sounds too good to be true. No wonder I was weak in the knees."

"What do you mean, weak in the knees?" A. J. asked suspiciously.

Now it was Lydia's turn to gush. "You said it yourself. He's handsome, nice, kind, and all-around wonderful."

A. J. suddenly hit the brakes and the little orange Toyota fishtailed across two lanes to a stop at the side of Mockingbird Lane. "Lydia, don't you dare."

Lydia was still gripping the dashboard and looking around to see what had caused their sudden stop. "Don't I dare what?" she gasped.

"You leave Eric alone," A. J. said angrily. "He's mine."

"Yours?" Lydia squinted at her friend in disbelief. "You mean, your boyfriend?"

"Yes. I mean, no," A. J. sputtered. "But I want him to be, so just butt out. There are plenty of other guys for you, so leave mine alone."

"But you hardly spent any time with Eric tonight. I mean, if you guys were so tight, why didn't I see you together?"

"Because I was too nervous," A. J. confessed. "I was shocked that he even came to the show. But I was feeling much more relaxed by the end of the evening. And I think if you hadn't have fallen, we could have had a great time at the restaurant."

"Oh, come on, A. J., you—" Lydia bit her lip, stopping herself before she said anything too mean.

A. J.'s eyes brimmed with tears. "I know what you're thinking. Why would a boy like Eric like somebody like me? Well, there's more to life than looking like a model and having to be the center of attention *all* the time."

Lydia winced. "Is that what you think about me?"

"Yes." A. J. jammed the car in gear and screeched back onto the road. "That's what everyone thinks. Lydia, you are so self-centered. I just wish, for once, you would think about somebody else."

Ow, that stung! Lydia decided she'd better lighten things up or one or the other of them was sure to say something she'd really regret. "I'm sorry you feel that way, A. J. But I'm a Leo. Leos crave the spotlight. I can't help it. I'll try to be——"

"I'm sick of hearing about you being a Leo," A. J. snapped. "Well, I'm a Capricorn, and we have feelings and creative thoughts, and need some attention, too."

"If it's attention you want, do something about yourself," Lydia shot back. She couldn't help it. What right did A. J. have to hurt her feelings? "I mean, you say you came to the party with Eric, and what did you do? You left him and spent the entire night at the hors d'oeuvres table, spilling food all over yourself." Lydia pointed at the ketchup smear on A. J.'s jacket. "Very attractive. That's a surefire way to get a boyfriend."

A. J. paled. She gripped the steering wheel and stared straight ahead. When she spoke, her words pierced Lydia's heart like an arrow. "You are cruel and selfish. No wonder someone left that trapdoor open for you. I wish—I really wish you'd broken your neck."

Lydia inhaled sharply. She could not believe what A. J. had just said. The girls rode the rest of the way to Lydia's house in a fierce silence.

A. J. didn't even pull into the driveway—she

just stopped the Toyota in the middle of the street. Without another word, Lydia pushed open the door and got out. She never looked back.

chapter 4

Uranus is putting on the brakes today.
Don't be surprised if something "leaps at
you out of the blue." Something totally
unexpected will happen. Could be awe-
some, could be a disaster. Play it cool,
Leo, and let your dignity rule the day.

Lydia couldn't sleep. It was her second night since
the accident, and A. J.'s words kept exploding
through her head like little lightning bolts.

No wonder someone left the trapdoor open for you.

Could it really have been deliberate? If the
open trapdoor had actually been meant for Lydia,
then whoever did it must have made sure that
Lydia—and Lydia alone—crossed the stage in
the dark.

Once again Lydia got out of bed. Maybe a
glass of milk would help her sleep this time. She
shuffled past her brother's room into the tiny
kitchen on the other side of the living room.
Saturday's events played through her head like a
music video on MTV.

First Garrett Hughes, the technical director, had stopped her on the way to the party. *Go back to your dressing room and get your costume. We're not your slaves.*

Sure, Garrett was a bit overbearing, and made no secret of his contempt for actors in general and Lydia in particular—but did that mean he wanted to hurt her?

Then there was Bill Glover, with whom she'd always had a love-hate relationship. He told her at the party that he'd left a small token of his appreciation for her in the dressing room. What *did* he leave? She never found out.

And Robin, for that matter. Hadn't he said something about leaving a bouquet of flowers from a "secret admirer"?

Thinking of presents in the dressing room, she remembered that the new girl, Paige Adams, had left a family heirloom—her grandmother's pin, or something—for Lydia.

And A. J., with whom Lydia hadn't spoken since their fight in the car. She'd told—no, *ordered* Lydia to go to the dressing room and get her purse.

And what about Keenan? Lydia took a sip of the milk she'd poured. *Ugh.* It was sour. Her mother had forgotten to go to the store again. Lydia poured herself a glass of water to get rid of the bad taste.

This is crazy. Lydia added the glass to the pile of dishes in the sink. *If I start thinking this way, soon everyone will be a suspect.* She shuffled back to her bed. *No one is out to get me. Bill Glover was right—it was an accident, pure and simple.*

Monday turned out to be as disastrous as the weekend. After finally getting to sleep Sunday night, Lydia overslept. She had been late to school enough times to know that her teachers weren't going to be happy if she did it again.

She bolted out of her house and made it to John Connally High in record time. She was without makeup, barely dressed, and completely rattled. So when she opened her locker and its total contents exploded onto the floor, Lydia slumped into a heap next to it, completely defeated.

Brrring!

"Great!" She stared miserably at the pile of spiral notebooks, old tennis shoes, and greasy lunch bags scattered about her feet. "Now I'm late for class!"

"Having a problem?" a deep voice echoed in the nearly empty school hall.

Lydia raised her head. *Eric. Perfect. First he finds me at the theater practically strangled by my own scarf. Now he sees me slumped like a slob in the middle of this trash heap. If he thinks I'm a total loser, I don't blame him.*

"Need some help?" he asked in a kind voice.

"Call the police, there's been an earthquake." She gestured weakly at the pile of debris at her feet. "Better yet, call an exterminator. I think some of this may still be alive."

Eric chuckled and dropped to one knee beside her. He was again dressed in black.

Hmm. Must be his serious-artist look.

"From the look of things, I'd have to say that you are having a bad day."

Lydia rolled her eyes. "My daily horoscope said something totally unexpected would happen to me," she said, thinking he would make fun of it. When he didn't, she continued, "I'm a Leo, and—"

"I figured that," he interrupted politely.

"That obvious, is it?" She winced at the memory of A. J.'s words about being self-centered, and hoped that was not what he meant.

"You're in the theater. That's the first clue."

"Okay, Mr. Zodiac, let me guess *your* sign."

Lydia thought about the astrology she knew, then picked an honest, straightforward sign. "Virgo?"

"Almost." Eric's grin widened as he said, "I'm an Aries with my moon in Virgo."

Aries. Lydia flipped in her mind through her *Love Signs* book. Aries was one of the most compatible signs with Leo.

"We're both fire signs," he continued. "Which means, I guess, we'd better be careful."

"Or invest in some flame-retardant outfits," Lydia said, with a suggestive arch of her eyebrow.

"So what *did* your horoscope say?" Eric asked as he started to collect some runaway pencils that had rolled across the hall.

Lydia looked at the ceiling and recited what she'd read that morning, finishing with, " 'Play it cool, Leo. Let your dignity rule.' "

"Sounds like good advice," Eric said, handing her the pencils.

"What it should have said is, stay home," she replied. "And pull the covers over your head."

"Hey, an overstuffed locker is not a cosmic problem." Eric was now busily trying to find caps for the pens that littered the floor. Lydia didn't have the heart to tell him that most of those pens probably didn't write.

"It's not just the locker," she said, grabbing her old sweaty gym suit that had never really dried and sat like a mildewing mountain between them. She quickly tucked it into the bottom corner of her locker. "It's the homework I left at home. It's the test I'm to take in romance literature that I know I'm going to blow because I haven't kept up because of all the time I've spent on the play. It's my parents fighting again."

"I thought your parents were divorced," he said, handing her two spiral notebooks from the first semester.

"Who told you that?"

Now it was Eric's turn to look embarrassed. "A. J. I, uh, asked her about you. Truth is, I bugged her until she gave me the briefest of details."

"Yeah? What else did she tell you?"

Lydia squeezed her eyes shut, waiting for him to repeat A. J.'s charge that she was selfish and cruel.

Eric surprised her. "She said you are a wonderful actress and one of the world's greatest friends."

"This must have been *before* Saturday night," Lydia said wryly.

"I think it was." Eric ran one hand through his jet-black hair. "Anyway, I'm sorry about your parents. Mine split up when I was seven. Luckily, I like my stepdad well enough, even if he thinks the arts are for weirdos and losers."

We're actually talking! Lydia was happy for the first time that day. *So I'm a little late for class—this is more important.*

"It's true," she said, tossing her tennis shoes, several leotards, and two pairs of socks back into the locker. "My parents are recently divorced. It wasn't pretty, believe me. Dad has already moved in with his girlfriend, which really burns Mom because she's still alone. Now we live in this dump of a house, since it's all my mom says we can afford, while Dad is happy as can be in his deluxe condo."

Motormouth! Now you've told him things you've never told another soul.

"My family sounds pathetic," she said, not looking up at him. "Sorry to whine."

"Hey, what are friends for?" He touched her shoulder and a delightful shiver ran through Lydia's body.

"Truth is," he continued, picking up a couple of old candy wrappers and tossing them in the trash, "it's a relief to find out you're human like the rest of us."

"Human?" she repeated. "What, you thought I was some sort of cyber robot? Or a windup doll?"

Eric's face reddened. "I didn't mean it to sound like that. Please, I'm sorry. It's just that you always seem so . . . perfect."

"You're not exactly a slouch," Lydia shot back. "Artist, poet, math and science genius. A regular Renaissance man. What do you do in your spare time, help homeless children?"

"Hey, this isn't easy for me, either," he said defensively.

"What isn't easy?" she asked, really not knowing.

"This." He pointed from himself to Lydia. "Getting acquainted. Trying to figure out if a person I'm interested in is equally . . ." He stopped and waved one hand as if trying to erase the last part. "All I mean is, don't work so hard at being perfect. A little imperfection is nice. If nothing else, it makes someone like you not so intimidating."

"Intimidating. Hmm . . ." Lydia cocked her head to study Eric's face. *He's not perfect either.*

That's good. He's terribly cute when he's fumbling for words.

"So, do you want me to help with the rest of that?" Eric gestured at the remaining trash on the floor.

Lydia glanced down at what was left and her eyes widened in horror. "Um, no—"

Too late. Eric lifted a crumpled sack lunch from the top of the pile. "And what have we here . . . ?"

"Don't," Lydia pleaded.

Ignoring her, he opened the sack and was immediately knocked back by the stench. He held it at arm's length. "When's this from? Last year?"

"Maybe," Lydia admitted, totally embarrassed.

Next he lifted a slightly damp, badly wrinkled leotard and stared at it suspiciously. "Ever hear of detergent?"

"Detergent?" Lydia pretended like she'd never heard the word.

"Soap for clothes," he said.

"Hmm," she said. "I may have to try it."

"No kidding," he said.

Under the leotard was all sorts of junk—student newspapers from last semester, old assignments, dance shoes, candy and gum wrappers, her old theatrical head shots and résumés, rehearsal schedules from shows long past, brochures for the Dallas Youth Theater that she meant to distribute but never did, and an orange that over time had shrunk to the size of a golf ball.

"Okay, you now know my most horrifying secret," Lydia said, wishing she was dead. "I'm the world's biggest slob. But remember," she added quickly, "you said you liked a little imperfection."

"A *little?*" Eric echoed, surveying the mess. "Lydia, your locker qualifies as a toxic-waste dump!"

"I have my good points, too!" she protested, starting to cram the stuff back into the locker.

Laughing, Eric helped her, stopping occasionally to toss old tests and long forgotten homework in a nearby trash can. They were almost done when Eric discovered something wrapped in a scrap of red material.

He shook the bundle and a small Barbie doll dropped onto the floor.

"You still play with dolls?" Eric joked.

"That's not mine," Lydia replied.

"It was in your locker."

"Maybe so," she said with a shrug. "But I've never seen it before."

He knelt to pick up the doll, which had been dressed in clothes resembling the red swimming costume Lydia had worn as Edith in *My One and Only*.

"Maybe it's some kind of opening-night present," he remarked, handing it to Lydia.

She turned the doll over and suddenly dropped it as if it were on fire. "Oh, my God!"

"What?"

Lydia covered her face with her hands. "Look at the doll, Eric!" she cried. "Look at it!"

Eric sucked in his breath sharply when he saw what had alarmed her. Someone had pierced the doll's stomach with a tiny dagger.

"Whoa. You have any idea who—"

"No." Lydia pressed her back against the lockers, trying to get as far away from the doll as possible. "It's like some kind of voodoo doll!"

"Maybe it's a joke." Eric picked up the doll and turned it over and over, looking for some kind of clue. "A *sick* joke, grant you, but a joke."

Lydia could only stare speechlessly at the mutilated figurine. When she finally spoke, her words were barely a whisper. "Like the trapdoor being left open? That kind of a joke?"

"Now you're making a huge assumption," Eric

said quickly. "Everyone knows that was an accident."

"Was it?"

Before Eric could reply, a door down the hall opened and a group of students wearing bizarre masks and costumes burst into the hall.

"What the . . . ?" Eric mumbled as they swarmed around the startled couple, making weird bird and animal noises and pressing in with their strange, monstrous faces.

Lydia realized in an instant what was going on. "Don't worry." She touched Eric lightly on the arm. "They're from my advanced mask-making class. We're studying the Italian masked characters from the sixteenth century *commedia dell'arte*. See?" Lydia pointed to the boy wearing a harlequin mask. "There's Robin. He's Arlecchino, the clever clown. And I'm supposed to be——" Suddenly she put her hands to her mouth. "Oh, no! Today's our final day. With all that's been going on, I completely forgot about it."

"My little Columbina!" Robin rushed forward and, taking Lydia by the hand, spoke in a phony Italian accent. "We were so worried about you. Little did we know you were out in the hall with a handsome Inamorato."

Eric straightened up, obviously uncomfortable with all of the playacting taking place. He backed quickly down the hall, stammering, "Well, um, speaking of class—I'd better get to poetry before Ms. Hubbard blows her stack."

"Wait!" Lydia cried. Things felt incomplete and weird. She started to go after him, but Robin cut her off.

"Let him go, Columbina. He means nothing."

"I'm not in the mood, Robin," Lydia said, attempting to push away and follow Eric, who was just turning the corner. Indeed, Eric was like the character Inamorato—good-looking, often funny, and, Lydia hoped, in love.

Robin gripped her arm firmly. "Lydia, it's a team project, remember?" he said in his own voice. "You want to ruin it for everyone?" Then in that fake Italian accent, he touched his heart and moaned, "Poor Arlecchino, he mees-es his Columbina."

Lydia couldn't stop herself from smiling. Robin always had that effect on her. "Oh, all right!"

She watched the rest of her classmates as they danced down the hall, striking the loose-limbed poses of the Italian theatrical characters. The voodoo doll, the tiny dagger still protruding from its stomach, lay at the foot of her locker.

Lydia quickly shoved the doll under some leotards and tennis shoes in the back of her locker, then raised up on her toes and knocked loose a box high on the top shelf. Inside it was her own mask, that of Columbina, a female clown known for her quick-wittedness.

She put the mask on and struck a pose. "You see before you a very different girl," she said, imitating Robin's Italian accent. "A girl with a secret."

Robin leaned in close to her ear and whispered, "Under ze mask we are all different people. With many different secrets."

Lydia kicked her locker shut dramatically and raced to join the others. *If I hurry, maybe I can catch a glimpse of Eric still walking to class.* Laughing gaily, Lydia turned the corner and froze—Eric was nowhere to be seen. *That's strange. He was just here.*

Before she could think any more about it, Robin took her by the hand, and the two clowns continued on their merry way.

chapter 5

Neptune's vibes are very colorful today, but very deceptive. Someone is lying to you, but it is such a sweet deceit that you are completely befuddled. It might be harmless, so don't blow a gasket. Just sift your information carefully.

"Can we talk in private, Lydia?"

Garrett Hughes, never the life of any party, looked grimmer than ever. He was standing outside the Backstage Club when Lydia arrived (late, as usual) for the regular Wednesday-night meeting of their theater club, Caught in the Act.

"Uh, sure, Garrett," Lydia said, walking briskly toward the big wooden door leading into the coffeehouse. "Maybe after the meeting."

Garrett put one hand across the door, blocking her way. "Not afterward. Now."

Lydia sighed in exasperation. "Garrett, you know tonight's meeting is extremely important," she said. "We're discussing the upcoming tryouts for *Evita*, which, as you well know, is only the biggest, most ambitious show the DYT has ever attempted."

"If it's so important to you," Garrett replied sarcastically, "you might have put out the effort to be on time. I've already wasted half an hour waiting for you."

"Oh, please! How could I know you wanted to speak to me? I'm not a mind reader—"

"Look, this is no time to bicker," he cut in. "What I have to say is very important."

Something in his tone made Lydia pause. Garrett looked very uneasy, almost jittery.

"Okay." Lydia checked the Swatch watch on her wrist. "But make it quick. I don't want to miss anything tonight."

"Let's go where it's private." Garrett took her arm and pulled her around the side of the building. "No one else should hear this."

"Garrett, really!"

"Be quiet, and listen." Glancing around to make certain no one was near, Garrett said, in a low voice, "Lydia, I've gone over and over what happened to you Saturday night."

"Don't tell me," she said, unable to resist mocking his seriousness. "You found the techie who left the trapdoor open and he's to be severely punished. No Twinkies for a week and a public thrashing at tonight's meeting."

Garrett ignored her sarcasm. "I'm certain someone deliberately left that trapdoor open for you to fall into."

Lydia felt the blood drain out of her face. "What makes you so sure?"

"Because, after the accident, I returned to the light booth to reprogram the board." Garrett took a deep breath. "I discovered the entire electrical system had been tampered with. Someone made very sure it would be pitch-black on that stage."

"But how could they know it would be *me*? Someone else could just as easily have crossed the stage and fallen into it."

"Yeah, I've wondered about that," Garrett said, nodding. "Lydia, did anyone tell you to return to your dressing room once the party started?"

"Well, for starters, you did," she said without flinching.

"I did?" He seemed not to remember.

"Right at the beginning of the party. You were very insistent that I return my costumes to wardrobe."

He shrugged his shoulders. "Me?"

"Oh, come on, Garrett!" she said with a sigh. "Yes, you."

"Well, I didn't do it!" he protested. "Who else?" he asked.

She was about to give him the list—Robin, A. J., Bill, that new girl—when she suddenly thought better of it.

What if Garrett is misleading me on purpose? What if he is the culprit, and pretending otherwise?

"Look, I promise to think about it and get back to you. In the meantime . . ." Lydia gestured with her thumb over her shoulder. "We're missing the meeting."

Before he could say more, she turned and headed for the door. Her stomach was churning, as if suddenly filled with a swarm of butterflies. First the accident, then the voodoo doll, and now Garrett's announcement that the accident was deliberate. Lydia was finding it hard to control the rising sense of panic inside her.

She opened the heavy wooden door and quietly stepped into the back of the meeting, which was well under way. The room was packed with most of the cast and crew from *My One and Only*, and as many others not in the last show who were interested in being in the next one.

Lydia scanned the room carefully. If what Garrett said was true, then someone at this very meeting had deliberately tried to hurt her. *Very scary.*

A. J. was seated on the side near the front. She spotted Lydia and waved.

Odd. A.J. hasn't spoken to me since Saturday night. And now here she was, signaling for Lydia to join her. *Maybe she's over it.* Lydia hoped so. She hurried to take the chair next to A. J.

In the front of the room, the club's treasurer, Corky Thoman, was giving a report on the club's finances. As he droned on A. J. whispered coolly, "I saw you with Eric. Did he ask you out?"

Lydia blinked in surprise. "No. He helped me pick up some things that fell out of my locker. Where were you? I didn't see you."

A. J. shrugged vaguely. "I was around."

"What were you doing, spying on me?" Lydia asked, half joking.

"Don't flatter yourself," A. J. muttered between her teeth. "The, um, principal asked me to take some flyers around to different classes. I was dropping one by Eric's poetry class when I saw you."

A. J. never lied. At least not in the past. But what she had just said was impossible. Ms.

Hubbard's poetry class was down a parallel hall from Lydia's locker. There were a dozen classrooms between them. A. J. couldn't possibly have seen Lydia and Eric together, unless she was hiding somewhere in the same corridor.

"Look, A. J.," Lydia whispered back. "I don't want to fight."

"You're the one who started this whole thing," A. J. replied.

Fortunately Robin slipped into the chair next to Lydia, which put an end to her conversation with A. J. His goofy smile told her that he, at least, didn't have a bone to pick with her.

What a relief.

Lydia smiled back at Robin and he draped a friendly arm over her shoulder. Trying to put Garrett and A. J. out of her head, Lydia turned her full attention to the new speaker addressing the group.

Marsha Boorman was the club's adult coordinator. She was on the DYT payroll as director of volunteers, chief fund-raiser, grant writer, director of public relations and marketing, and (she liked to joke) "head bottle washer." In fact, it was likely that the Youth Theater could not survive without her. Bill Glover was a good artistic director and, on occasion, an inspired man to work with—but Marsha did the better job keeping track of the money and bodies.

"Now that everyone's here," she said, "I need a volunteer."

"What else is new?" Robin whispered. Not content to share his flippant attitude with Lydia, he shouted, "What is it this time, Marsha? Wash the cars of the board members? Put fresh toilet paper in the rest rooms? Beg for money in the parking lot?"

"All three!" Marsha shot back with a smile. "Actually, all I need is someone to make copies of the scenes to be used in the *Evita* auditions."

A collective groan filled the room. No one moaned louder than Lydia, who detested what she considered "gofer" jobs. Her horoscope had deliberately advised Leos to avoid mindless activities. Standing in front of a copy machine and dealing with paper jams was, in Lydia's opinion, the height of mind-numbing tedium.

Lydia slumped down deeper in her seat, as did everyone around her, muttering, "Don't pick me. Don't pick me."

"Come on, people," Marsha pleaded, "I'm not asking for blood."

After a minute of excruciating silence, during which Marsha singled out and stared at every kid in the room, she said stiffly, "I'm disappointed in all of you, very disappointed. For your information, theater isn't a free ride. After all the staff and adult volunteers do for you, a little return favor isn't too much to ask."

A lone voice in the back suddenly said, "I'd be happy to help."

Lydia turned around in her chair. "It's that new girl, Paige," she whispered to Robin. "Paige, um, Adams, I think."

"Whoa, time warp," Robin murmured as he saw what the girl was wearing. Paige wore a sort of 1940s style dress with padded shoulders, her hair pulled into a clip at the base of her neck.

"She could be pretty," Lydia whispered back, "if she put on a little makeup and did something with her hair. It's almost as if she deliberately tries to disappear into the woodwork."

"Are you a member of Caught in the Act?" Marsha asked the newcomer.

"Not exactly, no," Paige said meekly.

"Well, I'm afraid I'll have to ask you to leave," Marsha said. "Invited guests only."

"Not so fast!" Lydia said, getting to her feet.

She wove her way through the chairs over to Paige. "She's my guest. I invited Paige to come tonight."

Lydia grabbed the girl's hand and pulled her to the front of the room. It had suddenly become very important to her that A. J. and the others in the club see that she was not completely self-centered, that she could care about other people.

"Marsha and everyone," Lydia announced, "please say hello to Paige Adams. She's new to Dallas, but is a real theater pro. We don't have time to go into all of Paige's credits, but most recently she starred as Dorothy in a national touring company of *The Wizard of Oz*."

While most of the group nodded in admiration, Paige said in the softest of voices, "Actually, I played Glinda the Good Witch. And it was a local children's theater, not a national touring company."

"Did any of you hear that?" Lydia asked, referring to Paige's volume.

"No!" Robin shouted from the back. "Come on, Paige, project!"

Project was something that Bill Glover was always shouting in rehearsals, so Robin's comment made everyone laugh.

"Hanging around with this bunch of loud-mouths, Paige will be bellowing in no time," Lydia said. "This girl saw every—I mean *every*—production of *My One and Only*. Which proves that she has excellent taste. So please, let's give her our warmest Dallas welcome."

The polite applause made Paige blush. "You didn't have to do that," she whispered to Lydia.

"Stick with me, kid," Lydia said, imitating a tough Hollywood agent, "and I'll make you a star."

"So, Paige, you wouldn't mind making copies of the script?" Marsha asked.

"I'd like to help in any way I can," Paige said sincerely.

"Well, thank you." Marsha smiled gratefully. "This group needs more people like you," she added, with a pointed look at the other club members. "And welcome to the Dallas Youth Theater."

"Come on." Lydia took Paige's hand again. "I want to introduce you to a few people."

As they made their way toward the back Lydia stopped to introduce Paige to everyone in the room. There were a lot of names for the new girl to remember, but she repeated them all, graciously telling every person, "Thank you for including me tonight."

Lydia felt good for the first time in days. She had taken Paige under her wing and people seemed to like her for it.

Returning to her seat, she motioned for Paige to sit next to her. "Are you sure?" Paige asked in her soft voice.

"Go ahead, Paige," A. J. said, getting up. "I'll grab another chair."

"Robin, meet Paige Adams," Lydia said.

"Hello, Paige Adams." Robin leaned over and kissed Paige's hand. "*Enchanté*."

Lydia was used to Robin's flirtatious antics. What caught her by surprise was that he didn't let go of Paige's hand until A. J. had returned with a chair.

"Don't let Marsha stick you with all the dirty work," A. J. advised.

"I stand forewarned," Paige said, warming up for the first time. "This is all happening so fast."

"You should try out for *Evita*," Robin told her.

"Yes!" Lydia added. "That's a great idea!"

"Oh, I couldn't." Paige lowered her long lashes. "I mean, I guess I can sing all right. But I just got to town, and the thought of actually being onstage at DYT—it's out of my league."

"Oh, don't talk like that," Lydia insisted.

"Everyone starts with a bit part. Mine was as one of the Lost Boys in *Peter Pan*. I didn't have a solo, didn't have a single line, in fact, but still I was petrified when we opened. By closing night, I was on my way."

"On her way to being a scenery-chewing ham sandwich," Robin kidded.

"You should talk!" Lydia shot back. "At least my voice never cracked during a performance."

"Lydia, please don't tell that story," Robin said, covering his head with his hands and wincing.

"You should've been there, Paige," Lydia pressed on, her eyes glinting with mischief. "Opening night of *The Music Man*. The theater is SRO—standing room only. Every critic in town is there. Robin was in the barbershop quartet. When his solo came, his voice suddenly leaped up about three octaves. Hysterical!"

"Yeah, really funny," Robin said, rolling his eyes.

"Oh, I would've died if that happened to me," Paige said sympathetically.

"What you need," Lydia told her, "is some confidence."

"True," Paige admitted. "Do you have some in a bottle I can drink?"

"Stop this right now!" Lydia put her hands on

her hips. "Promise you'll let me help you with your audition."

Paige stared at her in shock. "You'd actually do that for me?"

"I know what they want to see," Lydia told her. "A. J., Robin, we'll all help, won't we?"

"Sure." A. J. smiled at Paige, and even gave a friendly nod to Lydia. It wasn't as dramatic as a full smile, but it was a start.

"Absolutely," Robin added, smiling at Paige. "I know they'll find some part for you. Please try out. If only to protect me from the wicked and cruel Lydia."

Lydia's laugh caught in her throat. Was Robin serious? Did he really think she was cruel and wicked? *Now stop. You're just being paranoid.*

Paige agreed to consider the idea. Then Lydia, Robin, and even A. J. spent the next hour telling her everything she'd need to know about life at DYT.

Lydia checked her watch. "Oh, God. My mom's been waiting out front for fifteen minutes. I'd better run."

"You're leaving?" Paige asked.

"Got to," Lydia said, standing up. "I still have too much homework waiting for me." She leaned down and gave Paige a hug. "I'm so glad you came tonight."

"I owe my coming to you," Paige said. "I can't believe you all want me as a friend."

"Want my mom to drop you home?" Lydia asked, about to leave.

"Oh, I can take the bus," Paige said. "That's how I got here."

"Paige, you don't want to be riding a bus at this hour," Robin said. "I'll drive you home."

Perfect, Lydia thought as she left the coffee-house. *If any boy can make her bloom, it's Robin. And he's been wanting a girlfriend for the longest time. Who knows? Maybe something will work out there. He'll certainly help her spruce up her look. After that, they'll make a cute couple.*

Stepping into the warm evening air, Lydia felt happy, almost serene. It felt good to help someone. Especially someone new and so uncertain.

Now if only she could get A. J. to understand the situation with Eric. And call a truce with Keenan. She headed toward the waiting car.

"Hey, Lydia!" someone shouted from behind.

It was Garrett, chasing after her again.

"I didn't see you leave," he said, catching his breath.

"My mom is waiting." She gestured toward her mother's old beat-up station wagon in the parking lot.

"I know. I just want you to keep an eye out for anything strange."

She wanted to tell Garrett to leave her alone. To take his weird paranoia and bother someone else with it. But she was feeling too good to be mean.

"Whatever you say," she said politely.

Lydia said good-bye and ran for the car. It took a few minutes to get her brother, Jake, into the backseat and the groceries and herself into the front. When her mom finally pulled out of the parking lot, Lydia realized Garrett was still standing on the curb. Watching her.

Creepy. Lydia shivered again. *Really creepy.*

chapter 6

LEO—Feeling misunderstood by your friends? Perhaps it's time to clear the air—or make a new friend. . . .

Thursday, Lydia walked to school alone. This was unusual, as A. J. usually swung by on Thursdays to give her a lift. But today she didn't show. She also hadn't called.

I hope this day isn't weird. Lydia hurried up the front steps of Connally High, that confused feeling in her stomach.

Stranger still, when she reached the front hall, she saw Paige Adams. And Paige was talking to Eric. They were standing by themselves, almost out of sight beside the school trophy case.

"Well, look who's here!" Lydia remarked as she broke up what seemed to be an extremely friendly conversation.

"Hey, Lydia," Eric said with his charming

smile, as if nothing was unusual. "We were just talking a little astrology."

"Really?" Lydia said.

"I was telling Eric that my horoscope told me I might make a new friend," Paige said.

A new friend? Like Eric? Lydia put aside her jealous thoughts. "That's funny," she said. "My horoscope said the same thing. Are you a Leo?"

Paige nodded. "Just like you! Isn't that great?"

"How did you know I was a Leo?" Lydia asked, cocking her head.

Paige gestured casually to Eric. "He told me. What day were you born?"

"August sixth."

Paige's eyes grew wide. "August sixth? That's *my* birthday, too!"

"It's fate," Eric said, looking from one to the other.

"Well, that certainly helps explain why I feel so comfortable around you," Paige told Lydia, "even if you are a star."

Lydia ignored the compliment and said, "I didn't know you were registered here."

"Oh, I liked you and your friends so much, and you seemed so much nicer than the kids at Chisholm High, that I begged my parents to let me apply," Paige explained. "My dad pulled a few strings and got the selection committee to let me audition yesterday—and guess what?"

Lydia shrugged. The answer was obvious.

"Last night they called to tell me I'd gotten in!" Paige said, elated.

Lydia was surprised. Paige didn't strike her as the type to take the bull by the horns. And how did she ever find the courage not only to get up in front of a faculty selection committee, but be good enough to get into this special school for the arts?

As if to answer her question, Paige said, "I think they let me in just because a few kids had moved away. I mean, no way I would have been considered if I'd applied when the two of you did."

She's trying too hard to be liked, Lydia thought, *but I guess that's to be expected when you're new. Maybe my horoscope was right. Maybe A.J. is out and Paige is in. Presto! A new friend.*

Yet, for all her good feelings, something nagged at Lydia. Paige and Eric had looked pretty cozy together. Would a mouse like Paige dare to put the moves on him?

"Robin!" Paige looked beyond Lydia and

waved. "Wait up." She turned back to Lydia and Eric, saying, "I'll leave you two alone."

That's a relief, Lydia thought as Paige ran off to join Robin. Obviously, Paige understood the situation.

She turned to watch Robin mime being inside a box. When Paige arrived, he insisted silently that she had to "knock" to come inside to talk to him. Paige pretended to rap her knuckles on the invisible box. Robin opened an imaginary door and waved her inside, forcing her to stand very close to him.

Better yet, she's definitely interested in Robin, not Eric.

"Looks like those two are really hitting it off," Lydia said to Eric.

He nodded. "It's nice that two of your best friends like each other."

Lydia was perplexed. "Robin's certainly a dear friend. But Paige? I hardly know her."

"Really?" It was Eric's turn to be surprised. "From the way she talked, I thought you two had known each other for years."

"Well, maybe it feels that way to her," Lydia replied. "But I only met her last weekend at the cast party."

"You're kidding. She seemed to know so much about you." He shook his head and smiled. "Maybe you are spiritual twins."

"It does seem incredible," Lydia agreed. "Not only are Paige and I both Leos, we were born on the same day in the same year. We're exactly the same age. Though I understand that can make for a tricky friendship, especially when two Leos try to share the same spotlight."

"Well, that won't happen with Paige," Eric predicted. "She's crazy about you. But it's hard to believe she's a Leo. I mean, she's so . . . so mousy."

"And I'm such a nasty lion, is that it?" Lydia said, feigning hurt.

Before he could reply, the first bell rang, ending the conversation.

"Want to get together at lunch?" he asked, about to turn toward class.

"Sure," she said with a flirtatious smile. "What's the cafeteria serving?"

"Gazelle. Leos love it." Eric roared like a lion, much to Lydia's delight.

The day passed quickly. The gossip between classes was about how Robin and "that new girl" were looking like an instant couple. Lydia was happy to throw in her opinion that he and Paige were "absolutely made for each other"—especially as it helped steer any gossip away from Eric.

As she arrived for her last class, advanced acting, she realized that the only sour note all day had been A. J., who seemed determined to maintain the chill in their relationship. A. J. had avoided her in art class, where Lydia had hoped to clear the air, as her horoscope had suggested. Seeing each other in the hall between classes, A. J. had responded to Lydia's questions with the shortest possible answers.

Lydia knew the source of the problem. *She's jealous, plain and simple.* But knowing the reason for her friend's anger and dealing with it were two different things. She hoped that time would sort it all out.

Lydia took her seat and watched Paige enter the class and take an empty seat in back. She looked very nervous. This was understandable since the teacher, Zoë McGuire, had enjoyed a brief success on the New York stage and wouldn't tolerate "amateurs."

"I see we have a new student," Ms. McGuire said, studying a paper from the office. "Paige Adams. Are you here, Miss Adams?"

Paige timidly raised her hand.

"Welcome," Ms. McGuire said, managing a thin smile. "Do you have something to share with us?"

Paige cocked her head. "Beg your pardon?"

"A monologue," Ms. McGuire said. "Everyone else had to present a monologue the first day of class. Since this is your first day, it's only appropriate that you do the same."

"But I just got here," Paige said, horrified. "I'm not ready."

"You're not prepared. Is that what you're telling me?" Ms. McGuire leaned forward, staring at poor Paige.

Nobody breathed. Paige turned to Robin for help, but he lowered his eyes. Robin wasn't about to take on Ms. McGuire.

Maybe I should say something. Lydia was one of Ms. McGuire's favorites. Perhaps a word on Paige's behalf would help. Then again, maybe it was time for Paige to test her wings.

"This is advanced acting," Ms. McGuire informed Paige. "All students should have several monologues ready at all times. A Shakespearean piece. A modern, dramatic piece. And a contemporary comic piece. What if a powerful casting agent came to this school and expressed some interest in you? Being unprepared could cost you the opportunity of a lifetime."

"Yes, ma'am," Paige said stiffly.

Ms. McGuire was about to turn to other matters, when Paige raised her hand.

"Yes?" Ms. McGuire asked.

"I have a monologue I could try," Paige said, her voice betraying her lack of self-confidence.

"And what is it?" Ms. McGuire stared at her.

"Something I did last year at my old school," Paige said, standing up. "Emily's speech from the grave in *Our Town* by Thornton Wilder."

"I know who wrote it," Ms. McGuire said, not giving Paige an inch. "Well, Miss Adams, we're waiting."

As Paige passed her Lydia squeezed her hand for luck.

As if Paige wasn't already nervous, Ms. McGuire took a seat in the very front row. Paige faced the class, then took several deep breaths and closed her eyes, as if trying to remember a speech long forgotten.

"We don't have all day," Ms. McGuire said, tapping her fingers on the desk impatiently.

"Emily, now dead, is in the graveyard," Paige

began, setting up the monologue. "And she's come back to say one final farewell to her home and family and all earthly things." She turned and focused on a spot at the back of the room. Her face transformed completely from a plain teenager to a beautiful young woman. She raised one delicate hand in farewell and began the speech.

"Good-bye, world. Good-bye, Grovers Corners . . ."

Her voice was clear and powerful. All of the sorrow of Emily's short, tragic life filled the room.

Paige was mesmerizing. Her talent caught Lydia completely by surprise. *She's* good. Very *good.*

"Oh, Earth, you're too wonderful for anyone to realize you!"

When Paige was done, everyone sat in awed silence for a moment. Even Ms. McGuire wiped a tear from her eye before she uttered, "Thank you, Paige."

Then the class burst into wild applause. Lydia leaped up and hugged her new friend. "That was amazing," she told Paige. "Wow!"

Lydia was sincerely happy for Paige—until she heard what everyone else was saying.

"I've never seen anything like that before," Robin gushed.

"You are what is known as a natural talent," Ms. McGuire said. "That is very rare."

Lydia panicked. Her smile froze on her face. Could Paige possibly usurp her spot as the school's, and the DYT's, leading lady?

No. That was just beginner's luck.

Lydia knew that being an actress took much more than doing one good speech in front of a Texas high-school class. It meant going out night after night in front of a crowd of strangers, not just a circle of supportive fellow actors.

Lydia's smile began to thaw. *It was just a fluke.*

After class, Lydia led her classmates in complimenting Paige. It was all very friendly—until Keenan appeared.

"Feeling a little shaky up on that pedestal?" he whispered into her ear.

"What does that mean?" Lydia flinched away from him.

"Looks like you got more than a little competition," he said, obviously pleased with the development.

Lydia was about to respond when Paige stepped between them.

"Excuse me, everyone," she said. "I have a confession to make."

The room became silent.

"Don't tell us you're wanted by the police?" Robin joked, hoping to ease the tension.

"Not exactly." Paige smiled, appreciating his effort. "I want everyone to know that what you just witnessed was a pure imitation of Lydia."

All eyes turned to Lydia, as if somehow she was responsible.

"She's the great talent," Paige went on. "In my mind, I was imagining how she would do Emily's speech."

The look of total admiration in Paige's eyes was impossible to deny, and Lydia relaxed for a moment.

Not able to resist getting a dig in, Lydia motioned him back, then whispered in his ear, "You're just worried for your girlfriend Jill. Because now there's another blonde on the scene, and my bet is that Paige will give your girl a run for her money."

Leaving Keenan speechless, Lydia joined Robin and Paige and the threesome left the room.

"Boy, some debut," Robin said as he, Paige,

and Lydia left the room. "The perfect warm-up to Saturday afternoon's auditions."

"Auditions?" Paige asked, completely mystified. "I totally forgot about them."

"You should call ahead and reserve a slot," Robin went on.

"Oh, I couldn't." Paige looked to Lydia for support. "I'm not ready. I think I'll wait till another time."

That's fine with me. After her beautiful performance in acting class, Lydia wasn't about to encourage Paige to audition.

c h a p t e r 7

Red alert, red alert: Mars in retrograde has
come back to devil you a bit. Remember, it
isn't only knives that cut. Sometimes it's
tongues. Be on your guard!

Lydia—
have to work late. Microwave something from freezer
for you and Jake.

Love,
Mom.

Lydia studied the note left on the kitchen
counter. *What's happened to our family? No one is
ever home. We communicate by notes. And eat frozen
food. Yum.*

Grabbing an apple and a glass of iced tea
from the fridge, Lydia moved to the phone to
check the answering machine. From the flashing
red light, she could tell that there were two
messages.

She pushed the button to listen to the first
message and immediately recognized A. J.'s voice.

"Lydia, this is Anna Jo Gender. I'm just leaving DYT. They've posted the *Evita* audition sheets. I signed you up for next Saturday morning at ten-thirty—your usual lucky time. Please call the theater if there's a conflict."

Boy, A.J. sounds awfully formal. Hoping to find some friendliness in the very businesslike message, Lydia replayed it. *Nope. She's still mad.*

"Fine. Be that way," Lydia muttered, erasing the message and getting ready to listen to the second and last one.

For a moment she didn't recognize the male voice that said, "I hope I got the right number. Lydia, I, uh, was hoping . . . Oh, it's Eric." That was all.

Eric! Lydia was thrilled—and anxious, given that he had never called her house before. And his message. What was that about?

She punched the button to replay the message, which she did four times, if only for the pleasure of hearing him say her name. But even after repeated playings, she had no clue what he had stopped himself from saying. Was he calling to ask her out? And did he get nervous when she didn't answer? Or was he calling with bad news? Like he was interested in Paige, after all.

The suspense was killing her. But would it be too forward to call him back?

Come on, you're a Leo. Where's your courage? You know you won't be happy without Eric in your life!

Before she could pick up the phone book to find his number, the front door banged open and a voice called, "Mom?"

"She's staying late at work," Lydia called back. "As usual. I'm in the kitchen, Jake."

Her twelve-year-old brother shuffled into the kitchen. He was in his standard uniform: extremely baggy shorts, oversize black football jersey, and a faded Texas Rangers baseball cap. He clutched a skateboard in one hand and the mail in the other.

"Anything interesting?" Lydia cocked her head, trying to read the writing on the envelopes.

"Just bills. And more bills." Jake tossed the telltale white envelopes on the table. "Oh, and something for you." He handed her a large manila envelope, on which her name and address had been typed. There was no return address, so from the outside there was no way to know who the sender was.

Jake grabbed a handful of tortilla chips from a

half-empty bag sitting on the counter and waited for her to open the envelope.

"Do you mind?" Lydia turned her back. He was such a snoop!

"Must be your Tony Award." He sneered. "Or your contract from Steven Spielberg to costar in the next Tom Cruise blockbuster."

Lydia tore open the envelope and studied the single page inside.

MEET ME BY THE FOOTBRIDGE
IN THE PARK AT DUSK.

The message was clear, but unsigned.

Very strange.

Stranger still was how the message looked. It was a collage of letters pasted together. And it appeared the letters had been clipped from the DYT program for *My One and Only*. But it wasn't crude. No, it was definitely made by someone with an artistic eye. Someone who appreciated how letters looked and the words they made.

Eric! It has to be Eric!

As if she needed further proof, the site for the rendezvous—by the footbridge in the park—was notorious as a place for couples to meet. This had to be an invitation for a romantic evening. And how wonderfully mysterious Eric was being with this "secret admirer" approach.

Jake, who had polished off the tortilla chips and was working his way through a stale bowl of popcorn, mumbled, "So who's it from?"

Lydia pressed the letter to her chest. "That's for me to know and you to find out." She checked her watch. There was just enough time to microwave a frozen dinner for Jake, then hurry to redo her makeup, pick an outfit—something not too flashy, she was learning what Eric liked—and then run. No time for homework, which she knew she desperately needed to do. No time for more than a quick note to her mom:

Mom—
Meeting friends to rehearse. Will do homework later.
Won't be too late. Love you!

L.

"Look, Jake," she said as she scribbled the note, "I need to go out and meet a friend. I just remembered we're supposed to rehearse tonight."

Jake stopped chewing. "You're leaving me alone. Again?"

Lydia grabbed an individual serving of lasagna in the freezer and zapped it in the microwave oven. "I'll make you some lasagna—and I promise we'll spend time together tomorrow."

Jake's face registered his disappointment. "Why aren't you eating?"

"I've got to go." Lydia looked out the window. The sun was definitely setting. "And I'm not hungry."

The microwave beeped, and she brought over his dinner.

Jake poked at the lasagna. "I can see why you lost your appetite."

"I left Mom a note," she said, grabbing a brush from her purse and pulling it through her hair. "She'll be home in a few hours."

"Hey, don't worry about me," he said sarcastically. "I just love being by myself."

"I'm sorry, Jake, but I really have to go!" Lydia raced for her room and starting pulling off her clothes. She slipped on a long-sleeve T-shirt with little pearl buttons down the front and grabbed her pin-striped vest off a hanger in the closet.

Brrring!

"I'm sure that's for me!" Lydia charged into her mother's room, dived across the bed, and grabbed the portable phone. "Hello," she said, hoping it was Eric.

"Lydia? Are you okay?"

She recognized Paige's soft voice. "I'm fine." Lydia glanced at the digital clock on the bedside table. She had hoped to be on her way by now. "What's up?"

"Oh, I just wanted to thank you for taking me under your wing," Paige said. "You've been so nice, introducing me to your friends, making me feel welcome at school—everything."

"Look, you gave a terrific performance in Ms. McGuire's class," Lydia said quickly. "That'll take you farther than anything I might do."

"As a matter of fact," Paige went on, "I felt so encouraged by the class response that I'm definitely going to audition for *Evita*."

"Great." Lydia tapped her foot nervously, wishing the phone call would end.

"I'm aiming for something in the chorus," Paige continued, seemingly unaware of Lydia's urgency. "Nothing big. I already got my time locked in for Saturday."

"You what?" Lydia zeroed in on the conversation for the first time.

"I said I went ahead and scheduled my audition," Paige told her.

"Wow, that was fast."

"Oh, I was at the theater after school, copying scripts," Paige explained, "when the list was posted. Truth is, I was the first person to sign up—I hope everyone else won't jump to the conclusion that I'm way too pushy. I mean—"

"Don't be so hard on yourself," Lydia said, cutting her off. "You're talented and smart, and dedicated and pretty, and—"

"Pretty?" Paige repeated. "Hardly that."

"You could be," Lydia told her. "If you let yourself be. You should try another look for the audition."

"You mean, plastic surgery?" Paige joked.

"I'm serious," Lydia said. "I've only seen you wear your hair pulled into a ponytail. Why not try it down? And while you're at it, try a little mascara and blush. It'll help soften your features."

"Thanks, I will," Paige said. There was a moment of silence, before she said, "I'm sorry to be calling at the wrong time. You're obviously in some sort of hurry."

Cradling the portable, Lydia headed into the bathroom to do a quick touch-up to her own makeup. "Actually, I am meeting someone in a few minutes."

"Eric. Right? A hot date with Eric?"

"How did you know?"

"Oh, come on! You can't fool a fellow Leo." Paige chuckled. "Besides, you'd have to be blind not to notice the way he looks at you."

"I only hope you're right," Lydia said, checking her appearance in the mirror. "Paige, I'm sorry to do this, but I got to run. I was supposed to meet him in the park five minutes ago. Cross your fingers. If anything momentous happens, I'll let you know."

"Promise?" Paige said.

"Promise. Wish me luck!"

"Good luck, Lydia."

Lydia dashed to return the portable phone to her mother's room, then raced back to the kitchen. "I'm off," she called to Jake, who was finishing his dinner.

"I might as well get my own apartment," he grumbled. "I'm alone most of the time as it is."

Lydia felt a pang of guilt and for half a second contemplated staying. *No.* She shook her head.

This is too important. I'll come back early and we'll spend some time talking or watching TV.

She headed off down the street for the park, walking just slowly enough not to break into a sweat. She couldn't get Jake's disappointed look out of her head. *After Evita is over, I'm going to spend more time with Jake. I have the theater, but what does he have besides a few undependable friends and video games?* He certainly didn't have a family. That blew up a year ago.

Lydia entered the park just as the sky was darkening. She took the path running alongside the road that led to the footbridge, where she assumed Eric would be waiting. *Please, be there!*

As she got closer and closer to the bridge, Lydia noticed that the park seemed almost deserted, which was a bit strange. Usually in the early evening, even after dark, a few runners, bikers, rollerbladers, or dog walkers could be seen moving along one of the well-lit paths. But not tonight.

At last. Lydia spied the footbridge.

Squinting to see if anyone was waiting there, Lydia didn't notice a slow-moving car approaching from behind. The car had its headlights off. Its tires barely made a sound on the pavement.

Without warning, the engine roared, and the car shot forward—directly at her!

Lydia heard the screeching tires and turned. "Wait! Stop!" She held up her hands in horror.

The car kept coming. Lydia jumped off the path and bolted into the park. Surely she'd be safe now. She looked over her shoulder.

"Oh, my God!" The car had jumped the curb and was barreling toward her.

Lydia ran for all she was worth directly toward the lake. Still the engine revved behind her.

The water was dark and murky, but it was her only chance. "Help!" she screamed as her feet left the ground and she dived in headfirst.

Lydia didn't even notice the cold. Struggling against her tangle of clothes, she kicked and forced her way farther under the surface, praying that the car wouldn't crash in on top of her.

Can't breathe. Lungs going to explode. Lydia stayed underwater until she felt she was going to pass out, then she twisted her body upward, breaking the surface far from shore.

"Air!" she gasped. "Oh, God. Air."

Through her blurry vision, Lydia saw the cream-colored car nearly hit a tree, then swerve to avoid the lake and speed off back toward the road.

Maybe the driver thought she had drowned. Lydia suddenly realized that she was shaking, partly from the frigid water but mostly from fear. "Please. Don't come back. Please."

Sobbing, choking, and frightened out of her wits, she somehow managed to swim back to shore and crawl out of the water. She collapsed in the mud, hardly believing what had just happened. Her lungs burned and her body ached—but she was alive.

Lydia raised her head and moaned in the direction of the fleeing car. "You could've killed me!"

The enormity of what had just happened suddenly struck. It was no accident. Someone had deliberately tried to run her down. Lydia bolted to her feet. *Gotta go home. Gotta hide.*

She stumbled through the trees, whimpering at every snapped twig or rustle of a leaf. Now she was shivering so hard her teeth were chattering. She darted from dark shadow to dark shadow, trying to focus on something besides the cold.

Who would do this to me? First the trapdoor, then the doll, and—and now this! Why?

Where was Eric? Hoping to find him, she worked her way back to the path and over to the footbridge. But the bridge was deserted. Had he come and gone? Was he still coming? Had he seen what just happened?

A sickening feeling crept up from her very toes. Maybe Eric had never intended to meet her. This whole thing had been a trap!

Maybe it was Eric behind the wheel of that car.

"No!" she moaned into the vacant darkness.

But the strange invitation. He'd sent it, hadn't he? And the phone message?

In the distance, Lydia heard a car slow and turn around, and her pulse quickened.

Run home! She fled, as fast as her wet, aching legs could carry her.

chapter 8

The moon is going to make you quite moody today, if you allow it! Keep in mind that it moves on swiftly, and don't overdo the emotions without practicing an apology.

At school the next morning, Lydia was a total wreck. She wore sunglasses because the night before, after running home from the park, she'd cried for hours.

Although she knew better, she couldn't bring herself to tell her mother or Jake what had happened. She would have had to admit that she'd lied about the rehearsal, and besides, what proof did she have that a car had tried to run her down?

So, locked in her room, unable to quiet her mind, Lydia had stayed up most of the night. It had given her a chance to catch up on homework, which was the excuse she gave her mother at breakfast for looking so tired. But mostly, staying up had given her time to worry.

"Thank God it's Friday," Lydia muttered as she climbed the front steps to school. Only eight more hours and she could run home to the safety of her room.

Keeping her sunglasses on tight, Lydia ducked her head low and moved straight to her locker, praying no one would notice her.

The morning classes seemed endless, but at least Lydia managed to disappear into the group of students who were at school in body if not in mind. Luckily, on Fridays and especially as the spring wore on, the teachers understood that the end of the week was not the time to expect good work, or to start new projects.

By lunch, it appeared Lydia might escape the day as a nobody—until Eric spotted her sitting by herself under a tree on the school grounds.

My God. He's coming this way! Lydia looked around for help. Didn't he nearly kill her last night?

"Hey, where have you been hiding yourself?" Eric asked with a big friendly grin.

"Nowhere." Lydia was afraid to look in his eyes. She stared hard at the bottle of soda water and carton of yogurt in front of her.

"You're avoiding me, right?"

"Why would I do that?" she asked, still not looking up.

"Why? Because of the stupid message I left for you yesterday," he said. "Mind if I join you in the shade?"

Lydia froze as Eric flopped casually on the grass next to her.

They sat in silence for a few, increasingly torturous moments. Finally Eric asked, "Lydia, are you angry about something?"

She plucked a blade of grass and shredded it into tiny green bits. "Should I be?"

"No," he said firmly. "At least I don't think so. Listen, the reason I called yesterday was to . . . was to ask you out after the audition Saturday. I guess I was thrown a little, when you didn't answer the phone, so I started to leave a message. Then I realized that maybe your mom might get to it first, so I stopped short, and ended up sounding pretty moronic. Right?"

He could be so charming. It was hard to resist.

"You were going to ask me out on a date?" Lydia allowed herself to look up into his warm, brown eyes.

"Something like that," he said, moving a strand

of her hair back into place. "I thought we could go somewhere for dinner, maybe take in a movie. It's up to you. I really like talking to you. Listen, Lydia, if you already have other plans—"

"Did you send me something unsigned in the mail?" Lydia said, cutting him off.

"Me? No."

"Were we supposed to meet at the park last night?"

He was genuinely confused. "Lydia, what's this about?"

He's innocent. Nobody's that good of an actor. She waved a hand in the air. "I'm sorry. Forget that question. I think I've got some kind of spring fever."

"Oh, speaking of forgetting . . ." Eric snapped his fingers. "I almost forgot. I left something for you in the car."

"What is it?" she asked.

"A biography of Eva Perón," he said, standing up. "You know, the real-life model for *Evita*. I checked it out of the library and polished it off this morning before breakfast. I thought you might want to read it before your audition."

"Great." Lydia smiled at Eric. *How could I ever have doubted him?*

"You want to wait here or walk with me?" He held out his hand, helping her to her feet.

Lydia tossed her yogurt carton in the trash and together they headed toward the student parking lot. As they walked Eric told her about what he had read. "Eva Perón was extremely poor in her native Argentina. But by sheer talent and ambition she became a famous actress and then married a powerful politician named Juan Perón. He was elected president of Argentina in the fifties, but a lot of people thought it was Eva who really ran the country. It's incredible. The people loved her so much that they nicknamed her 'Evita,' and long after her death, many Argentines continue to worship her memory."

Lydia smiled at Eric with pure delight. Most of the boys she had dated hardly read the newspaper. Yet here was Eric, so excited about this book. "I can't wait to read it," she said. "She sounds like a fascinating woman."

"Reading it will help prepare you for the part," he said as they moved down a row of parked cars.

"You mean, if I'm cast," Lydia said.

"Who else would they give the part to?" he asked with a shrug.

She was about to thank him for his confidence when he said, "Well, there's the car."

Lydia froze in her tracks. Eric's car, a cream-colored El Dorado, looked just like the car that had tried to run her down in the park.

"Something wrong?" he asked, noticing the sudden change in her attitude

"That—that car." She was barely able to say the words.

"Pretty fancy, huh?" he joked. "It's a real dinosaur. You should see the interior. Leather seats, electric windows, and locks, everything. There's even a voice that tells you when you're low on gas or if your door isn't closed properly. We've still got a few minutes before the end of lunch period—want to go for a spin?"

"No." Lydia's voice was dull and lifeless.

"Suit yourself. I'll get that book."

"Eric." She forced her voice to be strong. "I don't want the book. And I don't want to see you."

"Oh?" He cocked his head in confusion. "Listen, if tomorrow night's no good, maybe we can try for Sunday, or sometime next—"

"Not tomorrow." She turned and ran toward back toward the school. "Not ever!"

Lydia's next class was advanced acting and it

took all of the courage she could muster to walk
into the room and sit calmly in her seat.

Ms. McGuire was in a particularly foul mood
and spent the first ten minutes of the class
haranguing the group about their chronic lack of
preparation. Then, instead of doing the scheduled scene work, she abruptly changed her mind.

"We're going to work on improvisation for the
rest of the hour," Ms. McGuire announced.
"Lydia and Keenan—you two will start. Here's
the setup. You're a young married couple who
are not getting along."

"That won't take much acting," Robin cracked
to A. J. Unfortunately, the rest of the class heard
and joined in their snickering.

"Come on, you two." Ms. McGuire clapped
her hands. "Front and center."

"Do I have to?" Lydia refused to budge. "Can't
someone else try?"

"You mean you're not prepared?" Ms.
McGuire asked sternly.

"Please, Ms. McGuire. I'm just not in the
mood." Lydia knew her teacher would never buy
that excuse, but she really didn't want to get up
in front of the class. *Not with him. Not Keenan.*

"Ms. McGuire?" Paige had raised her hand.

"I'd be happy to take Lydia's place if she's not feeling well. If it'll help."

"Thank you for volunteering, Paige," Ms. McGuire said. "But it's Lydia's turn."

Lydia twisted in her seat to look at Paige, who shrugged, as if to say, "Sorry, but I tried."

Ms. McGuire glared at Lydia. "I'm waiting."

Lydia had no choice. She dragged herself to the front of the room.

"Why don't you and Keenan take a moment and get organized?" Ms. McGuire told them.

As Lydia and Keenan turned their backs to the group, Keenan hissed, "What's your problem, Lydia? Is the queen having a bad day?"

."Put a cork in it, Keenan," she said quietly. "I'm not in the mood."

"Just because Jill is going to blow you out of the water at those auditions tomorrow doesn't mean you have to take it out on everyone."

"Jill?" Lydia scoffed, rolling her eyes. "That sophomore twit? Please."

"Go ahead, laugh," Keenan warned. "Your days are numbered."

Lydia felt ill. How could she ever have found Keenan attractive? And how would she ever get through this class?

Meanwhile another teacher stepped into the room and handed Ms. McGuire a note. She studied the message, then said, "Well, Lydia, this must be your lucky day. You're wanted in the office."

"The office?" Lydia said. "What for?"

"All I know is you're to call home at once," the teacher replied.

"Good riddance," Keenan muttered as she left the room.

Her anger seething inside her, Lydia stomped down to the school office and dialed home.

Her brother answered.

"Jake? What are you doing home?"

"Is that you, Lydia?"

"I forgot my stuff for gym," he stammered. "I was excused to come home, but when I got here—"

Her brother's voice cracked and he couldn't go on.

"Jake!" Lydia shouted. "Tell me. What is it!"

"Lydia, we've been robbed."

"Robbed?" She couldn't believe it.

"You should see it," he said. It sounded like he was crying. "It's terrible, the place is a mess. I can't reach Mom—or Dad."

"Did you call the police?"

"No, I called you first."

"Well, call the police," Lydia said, trying to be calm. "Keep them there until I arrive. I'm leaving right away."

Lydia ran all the way home. When she arrived, Jake was sitting outside on the front porch.

"It's too creepy to go in there," he told her as she bent over to catch her breath. "There are cops crawling all over the house."

"Come on, Jake." Lydia helped her brother to his feet and kept her arm around him. "No one's going to hurt us with the police here."

Lydia opened the front door and surveyed the damage. Pillows knocked off the couch. Videotapes and CDs strewn on the floor. "That's strange."

Jake nodded. "It's terrible."

"No, I mean the TV and VCR are still here. And our stereo. Those are new speakers, too. So what did they take?"

Jake, whose eyes were red-rimmed, rubbed his nose on the back of his sleeve. "They must have taken something, 'cause the whole house is trashed."

He led her to his bedroom, passing a police officer who was jotting down notes. Another officer was dusting for fingerprints. The intruder had obviously gone through Jake's room, because it was even messier than usual. All of his clothes had been dumped in a big heap on the floor.

"Anything missing?" Lydia asked.

"Not that I know of," he said quietly. "But I'll check after the cops leave. They must be finishing in your room. You may not want to go in there."

"Why?" she asked fearfully.

One glance into Lydia's room gave her the answer. Her desk has been overturned, its contents spilled. Her bookshelves had been knocked over. Even the sheets had been ripped off the bed.

"My clothes," she gasped, peering into her closet. All of the ones she'd worked so hard to buy were gone. The only remaining pieces of her wardrobe were a few T-shirts and some old skirts from three years back.

But that wasn't what disturbed Lydia most. It was seeing her carefully framed photographs from past acting successes all stripped from her shelves and walls and smashed to smithereens.

A police officer was sifting through the debris when she came in. He looked up and murmured, "Sorry you had to come home to this."

Holding what was left of a broken frame, Lydia sat down on her bed. "Who would do this?"

"Vandals, most likely. We've had a rash of robberies lately. Must be the nice weather." The officer motioned to her desk and shelves. "Notice anything missing? Jewelry, coins, anything of value?"

Lydia did a slow scan of her room. "All of my good clothes are missing. I think everything else is here." Unable to hold back the tears, she asked again, "Why would somebody destroy our house?"

The officer shrugged. "Who knows? A robber breaks in and, not finding what he's after, goes berserk and tears up the place. I'm sorry to report this isn't that unusual."

"A robber?" Lydia said. "There are things a robber would've taken—like Jake's stamp collection, the TV and VCR, or Mom's silver. But nothing's missing."

"Well, given the mess, it's likely that something valuable *is* missing," the officer said. "Wait until your mother does an inventory—I'll bet she comes up with a list of missing things."

"You don't understand," Lydia protested. "Whoever did this is after me!"

The officer studied her for a moment. "Miss, my guess is that you're just upset."

"You're damn right I'm upset!" Lydia said, her voice rising. "But that does not make me some stupid, hysterical teenager!"

"We see all kinds of weirdos, miss," the officer said, sitting down next to her. "Maybe this wasn't a robbery. Maybe it was some vandals on a spree. Maybe it's some sort of pervert who likes women's clothes. Maybe it was just a girl in need of an outfit for Saturday night—"

"What are you going to do about it?" Lydia demanded. "I'll bet you leave here and forget about us. Just another case of vandalism."

The policeman stood up. "We've called your mother's office and left word for her to come home as soon as possible. Believe me, we'll do our job. If we're lucky, we'll catch whoever is responsible."

Lydia nodded, wishing it were true.

"Your brother mentioned that your parents got divorced recently," the policeman said carefully. "And it wasn't exactly friendly."

Lydia couldn't believe her ears. "Are you suggesting my dad had anything to do with this?"

"There are no obvious signs of a break-in," the officer explained. "Which means either a real pro jimmied the lock—or someone with a key let himself in."

"Well, it wasn't my dad!" Lydia protested

"Maybe he's still mad at your mother," the officer suggested.

"She said, it wasn't our dad!" Jake joined Lydia, his voice shaking with anger.

"Then a repairman? Someone who was given a key?"

"Check with my mom when she gets here," Lydia said, taking her brother's hand and holding on to it for all she was worth. "But I don't think so."

The officer scratched his head and surveyed the damage. "It's a crazy world we live in. Especially for you young people. Anything else you wish to tell me? Anything at all."

"Yes! This is all a plot," Lydia wanted to shout. She wanted to tell them that it was just part of a larger scheme that included the trapdoor, the voodoo doll, and the car at the park.

But the police would demand proof. What proof did she have? The trapdoor could have been an accident. The doll could have been a joke. And there were no witnesses to her encounter with the car in the park.

"No." Lydia squeezed her eyes shut. "I have nothing else to tell you."

Where is Mom? Or Dad? Why do we have to go through this alone? Lydia squeezed her brother's hand so tight, her knuckles turned white. *Why can't my life be different, and all of these horrible things just go away?*

chapter 9

After the police left, it took several hours for Lydia, Jake, and their mother to restore some semblance of order to the house. When it was time for dinner, none of them wanted to cook. They were all feeling a little shaky. Lydia's mom suggested she pick up Chinese takeout and Jake jumped at the chance to get out of the house and accompany her. Lydia stayed behind, making sure to lock all of the doors and windows.

It was creepy being all alone, but she was determined not to give in to fear. After all, she was a Leo. Leos were known for their recuperative powers, and she was determined to recover from the strange and horrible last few days. Or else.

Lydia spent the next half hour carefully picking pieces of glass from her treasured pictures. Some of the photos had been torn and she set those aside, planning to glue them back together. Each picture held a special memory of a play in which she had starred. The memories were almost enough to make her forget what had just happened.

Ding-dong.

The doorbell brought her back to the present.

Its sound shattered the quiet in the house, and she nearly jumped out of her skin.

Don't answer it. Lydia's heart pounded furiously in her chest. What if it was the thief, back to take the TV and stereo and valuables he missed the first time?

Ding-dong.

Lydia crawled on her hands and knees to the base of the picture window. She stood up, carefully pulling back the curtain to peek outside.

Whoever was out there was standing so close to the door that she couldn't see them. Lydia ducked back under the window frame.

"Just go away," she whispered. "Please just go away."

The doorbell rang a third time.

The police. Call them. They'll make him go away.

"Lydia?" a voice called through the front door. "Anyone home? Lydia? It's me, Paige."

"Paige?" Lydia released a sigh of relief. She sprang to her feet and unlocked the door.

Paige was dressed in another peculiar outfit, a long cotton dress that reminded Lydia of something out of the last century. She wore a kind of turban made of printed silk that looked much like the style worn by movie stars in the thirties.

"Lydia, I heard!" Paige stepped inside and gave Lydia a reassuring hug. "Oh, how awful for you!"

Lydia stiffened. "How did you hear?"

"A. J. told me," Paige said. "She heard about it in the front office at school."

Lydia cocked her head. "News travels fast. Especially bad news."

"She said your place was pretty torn up," Paige said, surveying the living room. "But it doesn't look it."

"That's because we've been picking up like crazy," Lydia replied. "When I got home, the house looked like a war zone. I'll show you what they did to my room. I still can't believe it."

Lydia led Paige to her room and pointed at the stack of broken picture frames and torn photos lying on her bed.

Paige's hands flew to her face in horror. "This is just awful. You must feel so . . . so violated."

Lydia nodded vigorously. "Our house was messed up, but I'm the only one in the family whose belongings were stolen and ruined. All of this"—she gestured at her room, which was still mostly in disarray—"was directed at me."

Paige perched on the edge of Lydia's bed. "Who would want to do this to you?"

Lydia shook her head, feeling the ache in her throat that signaled a new flood of tears. She bit her lip hard, determined not to cry. "I've thought, and thought, and thought. I mean, sure, I can be pretty full of myself at times, and hard to take. But I'm a good person, Paige, and a good friend!"

"I know you are." Paige clasped her hands in her lap and leaned forward. "Lydia, is there anyone you might have hurt?"

"I wouldn't hurt anyone on purpose!" Lydia protested.

"Of course not," Paige said gently. "But who might think you had?"

Lydia wiped her eyes, taking a moment to consider this. "Well," she said, "I know that A. J. is mad at me. We've barely spoken since *My One and Only* closed."

"What's she upset about?" Paige asked.

"For starters, she has this major crush on Eric," Lydia replied. "It really got to her when she found out I liked him, too. We've had crushes on the same boys before, but this one was different. She couldn't handle it, especially when Eric started to pay attention to me."

"That can't be it," Paige said. "A. J. has to know a boy like Eric would never even notice a girl like her. And not just because you entered the scene. She's such a slob."

"Paige, I know you're trying to help," Lydia said, "but you don't know A. J. She's been a great friend. She's incredibly generous and loyal. Or was, until recently."

Paige shrugged one shoulder. "Well, even a good friend can turn against you. I mean, I've only been here a little while, but I saw A. J. blow up at Garrett at the theater over some unimportant thing."

Hearing this brought a knowing grin to Lydia's face. "Oh, there's no denying A. J. has a temper. Once, during tech week for *My One and Only*, when Garrett's lighting guy missed a cue for the fourth time in a row, A. J. went bonkers. She tore off her headset, jumped off the stage, and ran into the lighting booth. Garrett and Bill had to stop her before she tore the guy's head off. But that was tech week, just before opening, when everyone's nerves are frayed."

Paige nodded. "Of course. I don't know what I was thinking. After all, what kind of best friend would break into your house and smash your personal things over a boy?"

"Right," Lydia agreed. But still . . . She couldn't shake the memory of the look A. J. had shot her when she mentioned she liked Eric. It was almost—well, murderous. And what about the way A. J. had behaved at school? Going out of the way to avoid her. And even spying on Lydia. Just in case, Lydia decided she'd better find out where A. J. had been that morning.

Paige brought her back to the moment by asking, "So, what about you and Eric? Are things going pretty well?"

Lydia frowned. Eric's car. The same one that tried to run her down. Could he have trashed her house and then come to find her at lunch? *Too confusing. Change the subject.*

Lydia forced herself to smile. "Speaking of romance, how's it going with Robin?"

"Robin?" Paige asked.

"He seems pretty crazy about you."

"Appearances can be deceiving," Paige said. "I like him. The problem is, Lydia, he seems to be head over heels in love with you."

Lydia laughed. "Oh, Robin and I are just friends. We goof around, but I could never be attracted to him in a hundred years. Not that he's isn't cute—he is. And his personality is one of the world's greatest. But it'd be like dating my brother."

"So it's all right if I like him?"

Not for the first time Lydia noticed that Paige's eyes were so changeable. Sometimes lavender, or pale blue, they were now a deep cobalt.

"Hey, you don't need my permission."

Paige suddenly spied Lydia's copy of *Evita* on her bedside table. "Oh, look! You've got the entire script. Lucky you. I have the original Broadway cast recording, which I've played so many times I hear it in my sleep."

"I know. Isn't the music great?" Lydia said. "I just love 'Don't Cry for Me, Argentina.'"

"Oh, that number is so haunting!" Paige agreed.

"I can't wait to sing it tomorrow." Lydia hugged the script to her chest.

"So you're still going to try out?" Paige asked.

The question startled Lydia. "Of course. Why wouldn't I?"

"I just thought, what with everything that's happened, that maybe you'd skip this show and wait—"

"Don't tell anyone," Lydia interrupted in a whisper, "but I plan to make a grand entrance to the audition, just like Evita's at the start of the play. I'm hoping to borrow a costume similar to the white dress Evita wore on Broadway."

Before they could say anymore, the girls heard the garage door going up.

"That must be Mom and Jake," Lydia said, heading for the door. "Want to stay for dinner?"

"Thanks, but I'd better not." Paige followed Lydia through the house. "Although I'd love to meet your parents sometime."

Lydia stopped in the family room. "My parents?" she repeated. "My parents are divorced. My dad has his own place."

"Oh. I'm sorry."

"It's okay. There was no way for you to know."

"Well, at least you still have a dad," Paige added, almost as an afterthought. "Mine died when I was young."

Lydia stared at her. "Your father is dead?"

Paige nodded. "Car accident."

"But last week I thought you said your father was the one who arranged your audition for Connally High."

"Did I?" Paige looked startled. "I meant my stepfather. You see, after my real father died, my mom remarried. Sorry if I confused you."

"No problem. Look, are you sure you don't want to stay?"

"No, I'd better go home and practice my terrible audition piece," Paige said. "Oh, by the way, I took your advice—about my appearance. Tell me what you think."

Paige unwrapped her silken turban and shook out her hair. She'd gotten her hair cut. It was identical to Lydia's. "I hope you don't mind."

Lydia was shocked that Paige had imitated her so exactly. Then again, Paige was still a blonde and Lydia's hair was much darker. And a lot of girls were wearing their hair short, especially with summer around the corner. No way in the world would they ever be mistaken for each other.

"I'm, um, a bit surprised," Lydia said carefully, "but flattered."

"Oh, good." Paige sighed in relief. "Lydia, I know I'm an awful pest, but one more thing. You're so good with makeup, I was wondering what color lipstick you use."

"Plum red. Though with your hair so blond, I'd recommend you go with a lighter shade."

"Thanks." Paige moved to the front door as Lydia's mom and brother entered the kitchen. "For everything."

They said good-bye, and after relocking the screen door, Lydia watched Paige walk down the sidewalk.

That's eerie. Paige is starting to walk like me. It was the shoes. They were almost identical to the heels Lydia wore.

She heard her mom and brother call to her from the kitchen, but Lydia stayed in the door and watched Paige till she disappeared out of sight. She knew imitation was considered the sincerest form of flattery—but still Lydia wondered. *Could Paige be taking it just a little too far?*

chapter 10

You are in a critical trine pattern. Trines usually mean ease in dealing with life's situations, but this trine is in the fiery Leo (fixed and stubborn), the fiery Aries (cardinal and active), and the fixed Sagittarius (mutable and jovial). You hardly know which way to turn.

"Lydia! Wait up!"

Eric? Oh, no. Audition days were always hard. But today was particularly tough. With her house having been robbed and the weirdness with the trapdoor and the car chasing her in the park— Lydia did not need to see him.

"I'm in a hurry," Lydia mumbled, "I have an audition at ten-thirty." She had just parked her mother's car in the theater parking lot and was moving as quickly as possible to the backstage door.

"I know." Eric jogged toward her, gesturing over his shoulder to the red Subaru disappearing in the distance. "Once again my car wouldn't start. Luckily, my mom was able to drop me off."

"What are you doing here?" Lydia asked suspiciously.

"Don't worry." He chuckled. "I'm not trying out for the role of Evita." His feeble attempt at humor landed with a thud. "Or any other part, for that matter. I realize I'm not an actor."

She kept her focus on the entrance ahead. *Get to the theater. Go inside. Do the best audition possible.*

"Listen, Lydia," he went on, "since I'm going to be working on the show—"

"As what?" Lydia threw open the theater's door and stepped into the darkened backstage. She could hear the piano pounding onstage and one of the auditioners doing a shaky rendition of one of the songs from the show.

"Scenic artist," Eric whispered as he walked beside her down the hall to the green room. "Didn't A. J. tell you?"

"No," Lydia answered bluntly.

"Oh, well, it's true." He jumped in front of her, blocking her way. "Anyway, I don't know what I did to upset you, but since we're both going to be here at DYT, I'm hoping we can at least sit down and clear the air."

"I'm due at the audition," Lydia said, trying to step around him.

"I didn't mean right now," Eric said, letting her pass. "I mean—Lydia, will you please stop and talk to me?"

Seeing Eric only confused her. Right now she needed to keep a clear head, and feel good, positive thoughts. She did not have to have her emotions sent through a blender. Lydia took a deep breath. "Look, Eric, I've been under a lot of stress. And I think you may know why. Anyway, could I please get past my audition before you and I talk any further?"

"Sure." He jammed his hands in the pockets of his dark jeans and shrugged. "Whatever you say."

His warm, brown eyes were filled with embarrassment and hurt, and Lydia instantly softened. She wanted to take back everything she'd said and apologize, but a voice deep inside stopped her. *Get a grip. You've got an audition. Focus on that.*

Lydia touched Eric lightly on the arm. "Thanks." Then she threw open the door to the green room and went in.

The scene there was understandably tense. Some actors had their eyes closed and were deep-breathing, trying to relax and to focus. Less experienced ones were still looking over their printed monologues, no doubt afraid they had already forgotten every word. A few were on the floor, doing stretches, rotating their heads in slow circles, pretending that everything was under control. There was very little small talk and a lot of nervous pacing.

Lydia put her things down under a chair. She pulled a bottle of water from her bag and took a few sips. She checked her watch: 10:20. Perfect. Enough time to relax, but not too much time to start doubting herself.

When 10:30 came and went, Lydia wasn't concerned. Auditions, even the first ones in the morning, tended to run behind schedule. Perhaps they had begun late.

She decided to check the audition list to see who she followed. That way, when that person went in, she would have four or five minutes to really focus on her entrance.

"Lydia? What are you doing here?"

It was Robin. He'd been stretching in one of the corners and just spotted her.

"Is that a joke?" she asked.

"Hardly. I thought your audition was at 9 A.M."

"No. A. J. signed me up for my usual time, ten-thirty." Lydia tried to stay calm, but already her heart was starting to pound furiously. "Robin, you know that's when I always audition."

"But you changed it," he said, moving over to the bulletin board. "You put yourself down to go first, at 9 A.M."

"That's impossible." Lydia rubbed her temple where a fierce headache was forming.

"See for yourself."

The audition list was posted on the bulletin board, which also held other audition notices, scholarship and job opportunities, and the business cards of private voice or movement instructors.

Lydia stood before the board, staring at the white sheet of paper in numb disbelief.

9:00 — LYDIA CRENSHAW

9:15 — LEA DEUTCH

9:30 — JERI MOLEN

9:45 — VALERIE KEEL

10:00 — MARK ANDREWS

10:15 — SKYE SPENCER

10:30 — ~~LYDIA CRENSHAW~~
CHAD NORMAN

10:45 — JUAN PEELMEYER

Someone had scratched out her name! And moved it to the 9 A.M. slot.

"I thought it was kind of odd when you didn't

show," Lydia heard Paige say from behind her, "since you seemed so ready last night."

A. J. entered the green room from the stage and glanced at her clipboard. "Okay, folks, we're up to ten forty-five," she announced. "Which means Juan Peelmeyer, you're next."

"Wait a second!" Lydia said. "I was supposed to be at ten-thirty!"

A. J. looked up. "Lydia, where were you? You said you were coming at nine."

Lydia frowned. "When did I say that?"

"This morning." A. J. took a note from under the metal clip and unfolded it. "I have your note right here."

"I didn't leave any note!"

"It was pinned to my office chair when I got here this morning," A. J. insisted. "Lydia, you can't keep changing the schedule just because you *think* you're a star! You changed the time—I have the proof right here."

Lydia put out her hand, demanding the note. A. J. rolled her eyes and handed it to her.

A. J. —

Put me down for 9 A.M. I want to go first

—Lydia.

"I didn't write this," Lydia said, holding the note at arm's length like it was a bomb. "Someone forged this!"

"Let me have a look," Robin demanded, peering over her shoulder.

"Oh, Lydia, give us a break!" A. J. said. "Look at the handwriting. Look at that little heart you always use in place of a dot above the *i* in the name. You wrote it. It's your note."

"She's right," Robin said, studying the writing. "It's definitely yours, Lydia."

"Whose side are you on?" Lydia challenged.

To make matters worse, Keenan chose that moment to arrive with Jill on his arm. "What's going on?" he asked.

"Lydia missed her audition," A. J. said, "but denies it's her fault."

"Well, if you believe the queen, nothing is ever her fault," Keenan said with a smirk.

"Stay out of this, Keenan," Lydia warned.

"Listen, I need to get back in there," A. J. said, turning for the stage.

Lydia grabbed A. J.'s arm, hard. "Not until we finish this!" she said hysterically. "I didn't write that note!"

"Come on, Lydia, that's your handwriting!"

"It may look like mine, but it isn't," Lydia tried to explain. "Someone is trying to sabotage me."

"Lydia, calm down!" Robin shouted.

"Don't try to lie your way out of it," A. J. snapped. "I know you too well. What did you do, oversleep again? Just admit it, you blew it."

"Look, I'm here, ready to go on, as scheduled!" Lydia insisted.

"No, Lydia," A. J. retorted firmly. "There is no room for you. The slots are filled." With that, she pulled her arm free and turned to leave the green room.

"A. J., please!"

Hearing Lydia's desperate plea, A. J. stopped. After a sigh, the stage manager said quietly, "I shouldn't do this, but I'll try and squeeze you in at the end of the scheduled auditions. If there's time."

"Thank you." Lydia felt totally humiliated.

"A. J., I'd happily give Lydia my slot," Paige said, stepping to the center of the room. She was dressed in a long coat, which was odd, considering the temperature outside. "Really. I can't imagine a show here without Lydia. She can take my time. And I'll go later, if everyone isn't too tired."

Lydia was about to leap at Paige's gracious offer when she saw the faces of the people in the room. They were ready to despise her for bumping sweet, wonderful Paige.

"No, Paige," she murmured. "You go on, as scheduled."

"Thanks to you," A. J. said angrily, "we're now behind schedule." With that, she stomped out of the green room.

Lydia marched to the far corner and threw herself into her chair. "I don't believe this!" she announced, to no one in particular.

Those near Lydia found other places to wait. Lydia didn't care. She glared angrily around the room, furious that someone would try such a cheap little trick. Only a few people would have known her well enough to put that heart over her *i*. A. J., Robin, for sure. And . . . *Keenan*!

He met her gaze straight on, then pointedly draped his arm around Jill.

Of course. When Lydia and Keenan were together last summer, she wrote him lots of notes, all of them with a heart dotting the *i*. Lydia studied him, sitting so smugly with Jill glued to his side. *He* would *do something like this. Just to get me.*

A. J. returned, studying the clipboard. "Okay, Paige, you're next!"

Paige crossed to the green room door and dropped her coat to the floor.

"*Mama mia!*" Robin said, his mouth falling open.

The other students gaped in amazement.

Paige was completely transformed. She looked just like Lydia in full makeup (including the trademark plum-red lipstick), blond hair, high heels, and most important, the white figure-hugging, extremely sexy dress that was nearly identical to the Broadway costume.

"She *is* Evita!" Robin gestured grandly toward Paige.

Paige gave him a coy smile and a wink, then followed A. J. out of the green room onto the stage.

Lydia sprang out of her seat and gestured toward the door. "I don't believe it. This is just too incredible."

Robin grinned. "Paige looks fantastic, doesn't she?"

"Fantastic?" Lydia shouted in Robin's face. "She looks like me!" She paced the room, fuming. "I mean, that's my walk. My hairstyle. She's even stolen my friends. Am I the only one to see it?"

"Oh, get off it, Lydia," Robin said scornfully. "You're just jealous!"

"Jealous? Of *her?*" Lydia threw up her arms in exasperation. "Puleeze."

"I mean, just look at you." Robin pulled Lydia over to the full-length mirror set on the wall right by the door leading to the stage. "You don't look at all alike."

Lydia stared at her image in dismay. She had planned to wear a white dress, too, and had even told Paige her intentions. But when she had gone to her closet that morning to get dressed, she remembered the dress had been stolen, along with all the rest of her wardrobe. She'd had to borrow one of her mother's dresses and pin it at the sides.

"But this isn't how I usually look, you know that." Lydia could feel the hysteria rising inside of her. "Paige is twisting your thoughts. Like she's twisting A. J. and everyone else around here."

"It was your idea that Paige and I get together," Robin reminded her. "What's the matter? Can't take the heat?"

Lydia's head throbbed. Her hands shook from the anger she was trying so desperately to keep inside. "Of course I can take it. What I can't take is someone trying to become me. That was my idea to dress like Evita. I told Paige, and she stole my idea."

Robin stared at her like she was from another planet. "Lydia, I was wrong. You're not just jealous," he said, loud enough for everyone in the green room to hear. "You are petty, mean, and a total paranoid!"

People were staring at Lydia in complete disgust.

Lydia turned helplessly in a circle. *It's a conspiracy. It has to be.*

But who would lead it? A. J. Could A. J. have been so upset about Eric that she plotted this whole weird psych-out? First introducing Paige to Lydia, then having Paige take over her personality. But then Robin would have had to have been in on it, too.

My God. Lydia slumped in her chair. *I don't have any friends.*

Hours passed. One by one, people left the green room to audition, returning only to grab their things and leave. Lydia was convinced that A. J. would make certain that they'd run out of time before Lydia could show her stuff.

Finally, five minutes before the auditions were

scheduled to end, A. J. wandered into the green room. "Okay, Lydia," she said stiffly. "They've agreed to let you in."

By now, Lydia was a complete wreck. Her head still ached, she had sweated through her outfit, and her skin and hair felt greasy. She tried to pump herself up by thinking, *They've saved the best for last.* Maybe the day would have a happy ending after all.

Standing in the wings, she heard A. J. announce her name. In every previous audition, when A. J. walked by her, she'd whispered, "Good luck, Lydie!" But today she passed without a word.

I'm on my own, Lydia thought. She tilted her chin and threw her head back. *Fine. I'll show her.*

Lydia moved downstage center, smiled at the piano player, then began her well-rehearsed song. She was no more than one or two measures into the song when a loud whisper was heard from the wings. "This is terrible!"

Lydia stopped cold. "Beg your pardon?" she called to the wings.

"Show us something new!" the voice rasped.

Lydia peered into the darkness. "Who's saying that?" she demanded. "Who's backstage?"

Bill Glover, seated down front with Garrett, stood up and leaned over the lip of the stage. "What are you talking about?" he asked. "Lydia, there's no one here but you, Garrett, and me."

"But I distinctly heard someone tell me I was terrible!" Lydia said, her voice shaking.

"Maybe it was your conscience," Garrett said dryly.

Taking another step to the wings, she squinted at backstage. No one. Whoever had been there was gone.

"Lydia, if you're having a problem," Bill said calmly, "take a deep breath and start over. Take it nice and easy."

She knew what Bill was doing. He was humoring her, like he humored the real amateurs who had the gall to try out at DYT. She refused to be intimidated by that. She walked back to center stage, took a moment, and began again.

But it was no use. She'd lost her concentration. The pent-up tension of the past few days overcame her and she struggled to get through her song, dropping enough lines that she knew someone listening would think she hadn't rehearsed enough. She was almost in tears when the final chord rang from the piano.

"Thank you, Lydia," Bill said without a hint of sympathy. "You know how this works. We'll put the names of the people we want to call back for a second look on the DYT message line by tomorrow morning."

"Bill, I know it's late. But can I have another try?" Lydia knew she was begging, but she could see the greatest role of her life slipping out of her grasp. "Just give me a moment. I promise the next time I will—"

"That's all right, Lydia, we've seen enough." Bill rose from his seat and motioned for Garrett to do the same.

Lydia stood alone on the brightly lit stage, watching them exit through the auditorium. *Okay,* she thought, *this wasn't my best audition by a long stretch. Still, they'll remember my previous work here at DYT. They know what I'm capable of doing.*

She was still standing there, hoping for a miracle, when the stage lights went out. She was forced to to find her way out in the dark.

chapter 11

"Busy!" Lydia slammed the phone down again. It was Sunday noon, and she had been calling the Dallas Youth Theater's answering machine since ten. No doubt everyone else who had auditioned also wanted to hear if he or she had been called back.

Just when Lydia was about to start crawling the walls, she got through.

"You've reached the Dallas Youth Theater." A. J.'s flat Southern drawl was heard on the line. "Callbacks for *Evita* will be held at 2 P.M. today. The following people have been called back."

The list was a long one. A. J. started with the bit parts and worked her way to the lead roles.

"Come on," Lydia said, although she knew no one was on the other end. "Hurry!"

At last A. J. announced the actors called back for the role of Che Guevara, the charismatic and dangerous Marxist rebel. It was no surprise that Keenan was among the three actors called back for the part. In fact, this cheered Lydia, because it signaled that the DYT seemed to be going with its regulars in the pivotal roles.

"Now for the role of Evita—" Lydia murmured along with A. J.

"Jill Swenson and Paige Adams."

"What about me?" Lydia hung up the phone and dialed again. There must have been some mistake. She listened to the message in its entirety. There was no mistake. Only two actors had been called back—Keenan's girlfriend Jill and Paige.

"This is unbelievable," Lydia said out loud.

"What is?" Jake asked, passing through the kitchen.

"I didn't get called back for the play," Lydia told her brother.

"I'm sure," Jake scoffed. "You're their main actress. It's a total mistake. Call A. J. and straighten it out."

Lydia nodded. Of course it was a mistake. She had never failed to make a callback for a part in her life. She waited for her brother to leave the room and then dialed A. J.'s home.

She decided to give A. J. the benefit of the doubt. So when her friend answered the phone, Lydia kept her tone friendly, joking about how she hadn't heard her name on the list. There obviously had been some sort of foul-up.

"No," A. J. told her stiffly. "The list is correct."

"You're telling me I didn't get called back?" Lydia was trying without success to keep her voice under control. "Not even for some minor role?"

"If your name's not on the list, you weren't called back."

"You did this! Or Paige! Or you and Paige and Robin together!" Lydia knew she was ranting, but she couldn't stop herself.

"Lydia, get ahold of yourself," A. J. responded calmly.

"She put you up to it! Paige! First she stole my friends, then my look, and now she's got *my* part!"

"Oh, come off it!" A. J. exploded. "This may come as a shock, Lydia, but there a lot of actors who have as much, if not more, talent than you! You can't play all the leads. Besides, not only were you late, you blew your audition. You can't blame *that* on Paige. You can't blame that on anyone but yourself!"

The memory of the audition was fresh in her mind. Someone had whispered from the wings and deliberately tried to make her blow it. Could it have been Paige? *Of course.*

"Paige is a breath of fresh air in this theater," A. J. stormed on. "She's kind and giving, and everything you're not. And now you want to destroy her. Well, I'm not going to help you. You're just jealous."

Lydia was stunned by her friend's angry words. She hung up and bolted out of the front door. Lydia desperately needed to talk to someone—if only to confirm that she wasn't going crazy.

But who? She ran through the now short list of people she considered her friends.

Robin. We've been best friends for aeons. Lydia felt sure that, unlike A. J., when push came to shove, Robin would always be there.

Since he only lived a few blocks away, she ran to his house, hoping to catch him at home. She found him in the backyard, mowing the lawn.

"We need to talk," she shouted over the sound of the mower. "Now."

Robin pushed in the choke, killing the engine. "Okay," he said, wiping his brow. "What's so important?"

Lydia rehashed her fight with A. J., and told him her feelings about Paige. Robin, who before had always been a willing shoulder to cry on, was cool.

"It's not Paige's fault that they don't want you for the role," he said.

"Robin, I know this sounds weird, but I think there's more to Paige than meets the eye," she warned. "I think everything she does or says is a big pose, and I'm afraid she might be using you."

"Using me? For what?" he asked skeptically.

"To get to me," Lydia said. "I think somehow Paige wants to become me, play my parts—to have my life in the theater."

Robin rolled his eyes. "Lydia, we've known each other for a long time. I've seen you through some pretty weird situations, but this one tops it all."

"Think about it," Lydia insisted. "Why else would she cut her hair exactly like mine, wear my exact color of lipstick, the same heels and dress, and walk like me, if she weren't trying to become me? Robin, if you help me, we can prove it."

"There was a time when I would have swallowed what you're saying, and have done anything you wanted," he said coldly. "But those days are gone. Lydia, you're being ridiculous, and frankly I've had it with you."

"But I thought we were friends."

"You're right," he said. "We *were* friends."

"Robin . . ."

"Oh, Lydia, stop acting!" He was getting angry. "I know all about what you told Paige!"

"Paige? I didn't tell her anything!"

"You said you could never be attracted to me. Not in a hundred years. You told her I was like a silly younger brother that you begrudgingly put up with. You also said I'd never make it in the theater."

"I never said any of those things!" Lydia protested.

"Yeah, right," he said with a smirk.

"Don't you see!" Lydia ran her hands through her hair, feeling like yanking it out by its roots. "Paige made all of that up so that you would turn against me."

"She didn't do it in a deliberate way," Robin explained. "She accidentally let it slip. But it's true, isn't it?"

"No." Lydia shook her head, hard. "Not exactly."

"No? No exactly?" Robin repeated sarcastically. "Which is it, then?"

"I-I said something like that," Lydia sputtered, "but Paige took my words and totally warped them."

"Tell it to someone who cares." Robin restarted the mower and, once the engine took hold, gripped the handle and moved away from her without a backward glance.

Lydia left Robin's yard in shock. *Paige is more cunning than I thought.* Lydia could just imagine what she had said to A. J. And Eric. And everybody else.

She needed to think, to try to piece together the events of the past two weeks in some coherent manner. She moved aimlessly down the tree-lined street, not knowing where she was headed, or caring.

It's like Shakespeare's Othello, *she thought. Iago pretends to be Othello's best friend. But actually Iago is plotting against Othello all the time. He gets some of Othello's friends to start doubting him. Pretty soon, Othello is convinced that even his wife, Desdemona, is making a fool of him. And in a rage of jealousy and paranoia, Othello strangles poor, innocent Desdemona.*

"Paige," Lydia said out loud. "She's my Iago. She's trying to destroy me."

Lydia was so deep in thought, she didn't hear the car slow down behind her and lightly tap its horn. It wasn't until it pulled alongside of her that she noticed it.

"Need a lift?" Eric called from behind the wheel of an old green-and-white Volkswagen van.

"No thanks," she replied, glancing nervously at his van and forcing herself to face forward again. Lydia was unsure what to feel about Eric now that Paige had been revealed as her nemesis.

"Lydia, please."

"Eric, I'm trying to sort through—" Lydia stopped herself short as she realized that this car was very different from the one she'd seen at school. "Whose van is that?" she asked.

"Mine," he said apologetically. "It was given to me by my cousin Terrence. Okay, so it's an ancient piece of scrap metal, but hey, it runs."

"What about the car you had at school?" she asked. "The fancy one with the leather seats and electric everything?"

"Oh, that belongs to Paige," he said. "Or to be exact, her parents. When my van broke down, she insisted I borrow it."

"Paige's car?" Lydia repeated, crossing around to the driver's side of the van.

"Yeah, wasn't that nice?" Eric leaned one elbow out his window. "I mean, she barely knows me, my car breaks down, and she's there in a heartbeat with hers."

Somewhere in Lydia's brain a lightbulb slowly started to flicker on as pieces of the puzzle began to fit together. She swallowed hard and said, "This is really important. When exactly did your car break down?"

"Friday, I think," he said. "Yeah, Friday morning, just as I was trying to get to school."

"Friday morning?" Lydia repeated.

Eric nodded. "What's this all about?"

Lydia didn't want to let up. "When did Paige lend you the car?"

Eric scratched his head. "That same morning. I was legging it to school, carrying that book I wanted to lend you, when all of a sudden Paige pulled over and told me to hop in."

"She offered her car right then?" Lydia asked.

"Right. At first I said no," he said. "I mean, I hardly know her. But she insisted. She said I'd be doing her a favor because her father had to pick her up after school, and she didn't have a way to get the car home."

"So you didn't have her car before Friday morning?" Lydia asked.

"No," he replied.

"Didn't it strike you funny that Paige just happened to be there to help out when your car broke down?" Lydia asked.

Eric shrugged. "Sometimes fate's just on your side."

Lydia pursed her lips. Could Paige really have been so clever as to sabotage Eric's car on Thursday, and then conveniently give him a lift, and her car, the next morning, so that Lydia would think he tried to kill her?

It was tempting to add it all up neatly. But Lydia had no proof about any of the conclusions her mind was leading her toward. *Better to keep quiet about it right now.* She was not about to make the same mistake with Eric that she had made with A. J. and Robin. *Take a different tack, and see where it goes.*

"Well, Paige sure is a great person," she declared, acting brilliantly. "Not only is she cute and talented, but she's proven herself a good person, which is all too rare in the theater."

Lydia waited for Eric to chime in with his own list of Paige's attributes. But his reaction was one of odd silence, as though he wanted to say something but was thinking better of it.

Noting this, Lydia asked, "Eric, is something wrong?"

He took a moment before saying slowly, "I know she's your friend. But haven't you noticed how she's imitating you? Not just imitating." He struggled for the right words. "It—it's almost like she's trying to step into your shoes and—and become you."

"Oh, thank you! Thank you!" In great relief, Lydia leaned through the open window and threw her arms around Eric. "No one else believed me. I thought I was losing my mind."

Lydia realized suddenly that this was the first time they'd ever been this close. It was a strange sensation that took them both by surprise. Any other time she would have savored this moment, but too many things—scary, disturbing things— were happening.

She pulled back and took a deep breath. Then she told him of the incidents that had made her suspect Paige was up to no good.

"I'll admit that I really can't prove any of it— the open trapdoor at DYT, her car nearly running me down, my house being robbed—but I just know she has to have been involved. I mean, who else could it be?"

Eric parked his van and joined Lydia on the side-walk. The two of them sat side by side on the curb.

"What makes you think it's someone you know?" he asked reasonably. "It could be a total stranger. Which means it could be anyone."

"No, a stranger wouldn't know about the party at DYT," Lydia pointed out. "Or where I went to school, or what specific clothes mattered most to me. It had to be Paige."

"What about the voodoo doll?" he countered. "Paige wasn't even at our school then."

"Yes, but didn't she show up the next day?"

"True," Eric admitted. "And wasn't she at the closing night party for *My One and Only*? I remember you talking to her."

Lydia gasped, putting one hand to her cheek. "Paige *was* at that party. It was the first time I met her. Paige the wallflower."

"But could she have known how to sabotage the lights," Eric wondered, "and how to set the trap, in just one night?"

"But she wasn't there just for closing night," Lydia said excitedly. "A. J. told me Paige had come to every performance and had even been hanging around the theater, trying to get up enough nerve to talk to me." She rolled her eyes toward the sky. "If I hadn't been such an egomaniac, I wouldn't have fallen for it."

"Don't be so hard on yourself." Eric gave her hand a comforting squeeze. "Everyone bought Paige's act. Assuming it is an act."

"Then you still don't believe it?" Lydia asked, pulling her hand away.

"I honestly don't know," he admitted. "I mean, why would Paige try to hurt you?"

"Maybe she can't stand someone else having success," Lydia thought out loud. "Maybe she craves the spotlight more than any of the rest of us. Maybe she'd do anything to get that part."

"But to go so far as to . . ." Eric discreetly didn't finish.

"Well, she's gotten what she wants," Lydia said with a sigh. "I'm safely out of the way at DYT, and the part of Evita is hers."

"What do you mean, you're out at DYT?" Eric asked.

"I mean I didn't even get called back. Not just for the lead, either. For anything."

"You're kidding." Eric frowned. "Then who *did* get called back for Evita."

"Paige, of course," Lydia told him. "And Jill."

Their eyes widened as the same thought occurred to them.

"Oh, no," Lydia groaned. "If Paige was

demented enough to go after me, even try to kill me—would she do the same to Jill?"

"Get in the car," Eric cried, springing to his feet. "We need to find a phone. And get word to Jill!"

chapter 12

Eric waited in the car at the convenience store while Lydia phoned first Jill, who wasn't home, then Keenan. She quickly told him everything that had happened since the night *My One and Only* closed.

Lydia hadn't expected him to fall over and praise her, but she had anticipated a little gratitude for trying to save his girlfriend.

Instead, Keenan was furious. "I knew you were low." He sneered. "But to try and scare Jill away from callbacks—that's the most pathetic thing you've ever done."

Lydia was disappointed. "Think what you like, Keenan," she said wearily. "Just promise me you'll stay with Jill. Don't let her out of your sight."

Keenan slammed down the phone.

"No go," Lydia said, climbing in the front seat of the van. "Keenan thinks I'd do anything to get that part." She pursed her lips. *And, at one time, I would have, too. Well, almost anything.*

"I guess we could call Jill," she continued, "but I'm sure she'd have the same response."

"What time do the callbacks start?" Eric asked.

"Two this afternoon," she told him.

He glanced at the clock attached to the van's dashboard. "That only gives us a couple hours." He sighed, heavy with thought. "Well, maybe I should get to Paige somehow. Make up some excuse—I need help with homework, or something. See if I can get a feel for what she might do."

"No, you can't just talk to her," Lydia said, shaking her head. "Eric, you have to ask her out."

"Ask her out?" he repeated, not believing his own ears. "Like on a date?"

"If she wants everything I have," Lydia explained, "sooner or later she'll throw Robin aside and go after you."

"You want me to ask Lady Macbeth out on a date?" he said with a weak smile.

"At least find a way to invite yourself to the auditions," she told him. "Make her think you're really interested in her."

"Hey, *you're* the actor, not me."

"Eric, it's the only way," Lydia insisted.

"Well, I don't know about this idea, but okay," he said. "And you?"

"Drop me at home and I'll call A. J. I'll see if I can talk her into letting me work the backstage crew with her. That way I'll have an excuse to be at the theater during callbacks. With you, me, and hopefully Keenan there, Jill should be safe."

When they arrived at her house, Eric parked the van but didn't turn off the engine. He stared at the steering wheel, choosing his words carefully. "If we're right about Paige, and she is some twisted person who would hurt people to get what she wants—then we could be really stupid trying to handle this by ourselves."

Lydia nodded. "But if we call the police, they'll think I'm just some hysterical teenager who's freaked out because my house was robbed. And it'll be back to you and me—"

"The lion and the ram," he cut in, using their astrological signs. "Trying to take on the world."

Lydia squinted one eye shut. "I wonder what my horoscope said for today. It would be nice if it said something like, 'The earth will shift on its axis and all of those who were doubters will now become believers.'"

"Actually, we can check." Eric reached behind his seat and pulled out a folded newspaper. "Just happen to have the *Dallas Sun-Times* right here."

"You read the horoscope while you drive?"

He shook his head. "I do the crossword puzzle at stoplights and in traffic jams. And when this old van breaks down. Words are my passion, remember?"

And you could be my passion, Lydia thought, looking into his velvet-brown eyes.

Eric thumbed through the paper. "Ah, here it is. Leo." He quickly read the words to himself. The smile on his face turned into a frown.

"What's it say?" Lydia reached for the paper.

Eric snapped it shut and quickly shoved the paper behind the seat. "You don't want to see it. It's all bogus. Who believes in it anyway?"

Lydia studied his face. "You do, or you would have showed me the paper." Then she retrieved the paper and opened it to the horoscope column titled *It's in the Stars*.

LEO — *There is physical danger today if you act impulsively. You might drop a glass, fumble the ball, or tear through your exam with an eraser. Cool your jets!*

When Lydia finished reading it, she carefully folded the paper and tucked it back behind Eric's seat. "Well. I guess the good news is that this day is half over and I won't be handling glass or playing football or taking a test. If we can make it till this evening, things should be just fine."

Eric had been watching her intently, trying to read her reaction. Suddenly he leaned across the seat and pressed his lips against hers in a kiss.

A shock like electricity pulsed through her body and she nearly jumped.

"I hope you don't mind," Eric said, pulling back. "But you looked so beautiful, I—"

"Beautiful?" she murmured, still feeling a little giddy from his kiss. "I don't feel—"

"So beautiful," he continued, "I couldn't help myself."

Lydia's face was flushed with embarrassment. She wanted to throw herself back into his arms, returning the kiss. But the moment had passed and there wasn't time.

"Let's meet at the theater fifteen minutes before the callbacks are to begin," Eric said, checking his watch. "I'll try to convince Paige to let me drive her there. Then you and I can meet backstage."

They said good-bye and Lydia hurried inside. She dialed A. J. first thing. As soon as A. J. heard who it was, her voice went cold. "What is it now?" she asked.

"A. J., can we bury the hatchet?" Lydia crossed her fingers and lied. "I know I blew my audition, but I'd like to still be part of the show. Do you think I could join your crew?"

A. J. didn't buy it. "What is this, a joke?" she demanded. "You have never picked up a hammer, or helped with the sets, in your life."

Try a new tactic. "Okay, A. J. Look, I would just like to come to the theater today to talk to you."

"Why? To tell me I'm stupid, and ugly?" A. J. interrupted. "Don't bother. I already heard."

"Who said that?" Lydia demanded.

"You did! That was a direct quote." A. J. bit off her words angrily. "Let's see, what else did you tell Paige. Oh, I remember—that Eric would rather die than go out with me. And everything I've accomplished I owe to you. I also let my parents run my life, but maybe that's a good idea since I'm incapable of doing it myself!"

"A. J., will you stop?" Lydia protested. "I never said those things. Don't you get it? It's Paige. She's been spreading lies, trying to get you to turn against me. She—"

A. J. cut her off. "Paige said you'd probably do this."

"Do what?"

"Try and blame it on her. Boy, has she got you figured out."

Swallowing her own hurt, Lydia calmly said, "I know your feelings are hurt, A. J. But I didn't say any of that. I want you to know that I still think of you as my best friend, even if you don't feel the same way."

A. J. said nothing.

Lydia forced herself to stick to her reason for calling. "A. J., please keep an eye on Paige today and don't let Jill out of your sight. I'm afraid something terrible could happen."

A. J. responded the way Lydia thought she would. She hung up.

Great.

Lydia slumped against the kitchen counter, filled with self-doubts. *Maybe I am losing my mind.*

Maybe I did say those words. I mean, the few times I've been angry with A.J., I've certainly thought a few of those things. Same goes with Robin. And that note did look like my handwriting. . . .

Brrring!

Luckily for Lydia, it was Eric. Saved by the phone.

"How'd it go with A. J.?" he asked.

"She hates me," Lydia confessed. "And no way will she let be me on any crew."

"I'm sorry. But we'll get this straightened out," he assured her.

"I wish I had your confidence."

"Well, I did my part," Eric reported. "I called Paige. I have to tell you, Lydia, if we ever doubted whether she was a slime, she proved it. She told me, for starters, that she was hoping that I'd call. After all of the things that you, Lydia, had said about me, she knew I'd need someone to talk to."

Not you, too. Lydia could barely bring herself to ask, "Did you believe her?"

"Of course not. I went along but only to fool her. She is one scary piece of work!"

Lydia closed her eyes, sighing in relief. "She's unbelievable."

"I suggested I give her a lift to callbacks, telling her I owed her a favor and that I had to be at DYT for a design meeting—which is a lie, by the way. She said she was just going out the door because her audition was scheduled for three-fifteen. In order to delay her, I had to lay it on pretty thick about how talented she was, and how I wanted to go out with her."

"So what happened?"

"She finally gave in. Then she told me her house was being painted and her parents didn't want any friends to see the mess, so we arranged to meet at the school parking lot at two forty-five."

Lydia glanced at her watch. "That's in fifteen minutes. You'd better go. I'll leave now and meet you backstage before three-thirty."

"At the far right corner," he added. "Precisely at three-fifteen. Be there. And be careful."

"Forget careful," Lydia said. "Let's both be lucky."

Lydia borrowed her mother's car and drove to the theater. She kept her thoughts positive.

Eric and I will stop this madness. Together we'll find a way to keep Jill from being hurt and put an end to all of this.

It was a glaringly sunny Dallas afternoon, very

warm for spring, when Lydia opened the stage door and stepped into the pitch-black theater.

She took a moment so her eyes could adjust to the lack of light. The last thing she wanted was to knock something over and be thrown out of the theater.

She silently wove her way between set pieces stored from previous DYT productions, heading for the corner where she was to meet Eric.

He hadn't arrived yet. She turned her watch in the direction of the light coming from the stage. *Three-thirteen, and counting.* Lydia stepped back into the darkness and listened to the auditions happening onstage.

She recognized Keenan's voice, He was reading for the role of Che and, by the sound of it, doing very well. Lydia heard Bill Glover give him some directions and ask him to read it a second time. His second reading was even better than his first. He was a cinch for the male lead.

Lydia leaned into the light to look at her watch: 3:20. Eric was late. *Where is he?*

Maybe she hadn't heard him correctly. Maybe he'd meant the right corner toward the front. She started to tiptoe in that direction, but stopped short. *Jill.*

The pretty blond stood in the opposite wings, watching Keenan perform. She was smiling, completely enraptured. Lydia smiled ruefully. She understood how Jill felt. After all, that's how she had been only last summer.

Lydia checked her watch again. Another five minutes had passed. *Could something have happened to Eric?*

Her foot bumped a piece of scenery. Her first urge was to retreat to the darkest corner. But just as she was about to take a step, she saw something move in the darkness behind Jill.

Someone was fiddling with the ropes that lowered and raised the sets.

It's just one of Garrett's backstage crew, Lydia concluded. *No.* This was a blond girl. With a very familiar haircut. *Paige!*

From across the stage, Lydia saw the rope Paige was loosening. The rope stretched to the grid on the ceiling, where it attached to a sandbag. The sandbag hung directly above Jill's head!

Lydia's heart thumped wildly in her chest. *I can't wait for Eric. I just can't wait!* Lydia bolted out of the wings onto the stage. She didn't stop to explain to Keenan or Bill. There wasn't time.

"What are you trying——?" Keenan shouted, perplexed.

"Lydia, please, you have no business being here!" Bill shouted.

"Hey, get off the stage!" Garrett screamed.

Lydia ducked her head low, ran past Jill, and hurled herself at Paige. They hit the ground with Lydia on top. But Paige was stronger than Lydia imagined. In a heartbeat, they'd flipped over and Lydia found herself staring up at the sandbag Paige had planned to drop on Jill. It swung wildly back and forth.

Jill screamed as she watched Lydia and Paige claw and scratch at each other. Paige grabbed Lydia by the hair and slammed her head hard against the wooden floor.

Lydia saw stars and, for a moment, thought she might pass out. With every ounce of strength she could muster, she heaved Paige off of her.

"Call the police," Lydia rasped, scrambling to her feet. Jill stood paralyzed with fear.

Paige found a long-handled wrench and swung it wildly at Lydia. "Get out," she growled. "Get out of my way."

Lydia caught the end of the wrench and the girls collided into the metal stand where the ropes for the counterweight system were tied off.

Paige looked up, wild-eyed, and suddenly shoved Lydia into Jill. The girl tumbled backward as Lydia fell to the ground, right on the spot where Jill had been standing.

Badly shaken, her breath knocked from her, Lydia looked up to see the sandbag hurtling toward her.

chapter 13

If you get to the end of the rainbow and find only a pot of beans—remember to take them home and plant them. What looks like a disappointment today will actually be a bonus of some sort. It may be money (Venus in nice aspect to Jupiter) or it may be just a lovely compliment from a friend.

For three weeks there was no light or dreams, only voices. Faint voices that crept into Lydia's injured brain: sometimes they were Paige's mocking cries of victory, other times they were her mother's worried moans; most often, they were Lydia's own voice asking, "Why . . . why?"

She had no idea if she was alive or dead. *Is this death,* she wondered during one of her few moments of clarity, *the mind going its eternal way while the body is no more?*

Unable to open her eyes, being fed by a tube in her arm, Lydia slept and slept, like the princess in the old stories waiting to be awakened by a prince's kiss.

"Lydia . . . Lydia . . ." The voice belonged to a

boy, but in her fog she could not tell exactly who.

"Lydia, please."

She sensed that he had been talking to her for a while, his gentle voice trying to float her to the surface.

"Lydia, please wake up," the voice continued. "I can't stand seeing you so still."

Lydia's closed eyelids fluttered slightly. *Come on!* Her mind was starting to clear. *You can do it!*

"That a girl!" the voice encouraged. "Lydia, you're a Leo, you're a fighter—now prove it! Prove it to everyone who ever doubted you!"

Lydia's mind was moving through thick layers of mental clouds.

She felt something—someone—take her hand and squeeze it gently. It was the first physical sensation she remembered feeling since the moment when everything went black.

Lydia let her eyelids cautiously separate, and then tried to focus. She wanted to force the most basic question from her throat—"Where am I?"—but she could not produce a single word.

A moment or two later her eyes adjusted to the low light in the room, and she could finally see the boy sitting by her bed. *Eric!*

"You're awake," he said hoarsely. "Lydia, you woke up!"

Lydia couldn't talk yet. She had to content herself with looking around. She definitely wasn't home, she was in a hospital. From the looks of all the fancy machines and monitors surrounding her bed, something had gone terribly wrong.

"What . . . what happened?" she managed to whisper. The words felt too thick for her throat, and she was suddenly aware of the terribly sour taste in her mouth.

"Don't try and talk," he told her.

But she had to know. "Eric, tell me," Lydia said in a haltingly slow voice, as if she were speaking a foreign language for the first time.

"I can't believe you're finally awake!" His voice was excited, like a kid at a birthday party. "I'd better go and tell the nurse!"

"Wait," she told him, "not yet." The words were still coming with difficulty, as if she had to remember how to form them. "Eric, how . . . how long?"

"By my count, you've been lost to the world for a lifetime." He smiled and added, "But by the calendar, almost three weeks."

"Three weeks?" Lydia said, trying to make sense of his answer. "Three weeks?"

She closed her eyes again, wanting to return to the safety of sleep.

Eric shook her gently, saying, "Lydia, don't go away! Come on, stay awake!"

Three weeks. Is that possible?

"Mrs. Bernard? Nurse?" Eric was at the door. "She's awake. Come quick!"

Lydia struggled to sit up and was instantly hit with the worst headache. Instinctively, she raised a hand to her head—and, to her shock, found it wrapped with heavy bandages.

She was filled with instant panic. "Eric? What is this?"

"You don't remember?"

"No."

"You don't remember anything?" he asked.

Lydia waited for the intense pain in her head to subside. She'd never felt anything so punishing in her life.

Speaking very slowly, she said, "I remember the theater. Someone screaming," she said, forcing the images to the surface. "And . . . that's all. Please tell me what happened."

Eric waved to the nurse in the hall and turned

to Lydia. "The nurse is coming. And she looks very happy. But not as happy as I feel."

"Please." Lydia's throat was parched. "Tell me what happened."

"You were hit in the head by a sandbag from the theater's counterweight system. It nearly crushed your skull." He shook his head. "You're lucky to be alive. And it's a miracle that you can still move your arms and legs."

"Well, welcome back, stranger!" A woman in a white uniform smiled from the doorway. She checked the monitors above Lydia's bed and pulled a penlight out of her pocket. "Do you know where you are?"

"I'm in a hospital. I don't know which one," Lydia replied. The nurse aimed the light first at one eye and then the other, checking her pupils.

"You had a pretty nasty bump on the head," the nurse said, checking her pulse. "How do you feel?"

"I'm not sure," Lydia replied, in barely a whisper. "I know I have a very bad headache and my mouth feels drier than the Sahara Desert."

"I think we can do something about both of those problems." The nurse, whose name tag said KATHRYN BERNARD, made a notation on her clipboard. "I'm going to call your doctor. He'll need to do a neurological exam. While I call, I'll bet Eric here would be more than happy to pour you a glass of water."

"My pleasure." Eric poured Lydia a drink from the pitcher of water that sat on her bedside table. He gently held the glass to her lips.

"Don't try to drink it at first," cautioned the nurse from the doorway. "Just moisten your lips a bit. We don't want to rush things. I'll be back in a second."

The liquid felt amazingly wonderful on her tongue, the best thing Lydia had ever tasted. "Thank you." She sighed. "Now tell me what happened at the theater. Please."

"Well, there was a lot of confusion, understandably," he said. "But someone—I think it was Garrett—called nine-one-one. They rushed you to the emergency room, and then into surgery."

Lydia raised one hand to touch her bandages. "I must look terrible."

"Not to me." Eric perched on the side of her bed, smiling at her. "In fact, I'd have to say that you look truly wonderful."

Lydia's headache throbbed again and she winced. "Am I going to be okay?"

"Of course." Eric caressed her cheek.

"Besides, it'd take more than a couple pounds of sand to get rid of you."

This caused her to smile for the first time since that horrible day. As her mind cleared she began to vaguely remember the events leading up to her injury.

"I was waiting backstage," she said, forcing her mind to concentrate. "Waiting for you."

"I know," he said, embarrassed.

"Where were you?"

"You may not remember, but that afternoon I told you on the phone that Paige hesitated for a second before she accepted my offer to give her a ride to the theater. Well, I must have said something that gave me away. The upshot is that Paige told me to meet her in the school parking lot. When I pulled in, every tire on my car went flat. I stepped out to find that the entrance had been covered with small steel tacks." He shook his head, still angry at himself. "By the time I got to the theater, they were taking you away in an ambulance."

Lydia closed her eyes. "I saw Paige trying to hurt Jill, and tried to stop her. Did they arrest Paige?"

Eric's face darkened. "Here's the really bad

news. Jill thought you were trying to hurt her. So did Keenan and, I'm afraid, A. J., and even Robin."

"You're joking?" Lydia said, alarmed.

"I wish I was," he said. "Garrett insisted they had it wrong, that you were the intended victim all along—"

"Garrett?" Lydia shook her head.

Eric nodded. "He's actually come by to visit a number of times. He said he knew someone was out to get you since the closing-night party for *My One and Only*—"

"He tried to warn me," Lydia said. "Only I wouldn't take him seriously."

"Neither did anyone else." Eric ran one hand through his hair. "The long and the short of it is, everyone thinks Paige was the hero who stopped you."

"This *is* a bad dream," Lydia moaned.

"Jill saw you dash across the stage and charge into Paige. But it was dark in the wings, and Jill couldn't swear what happened next, or why. She saw you and Paige struggling, and the sandbag was falling."

Lydia put her hand to her temple and rubbed it in a small circle. "So now Paige is telling everyone I tried to kill her?"

Eric shook his head. "Paige isn't telling anyone anything. She disappeared the next day."

"Disappeared?" Lydia repeated.

"Without a trace." Eric stood up and paced around the tiny hospital room. "It makes me so mad. I tried to get the police to find her. But they weren't interested, so I looked into it myself." He returned to Lydia's bedside. "I can't prove it, but I think Paige was here in Dallas on her own."

"But what about her parents?" Lydia asked, taking another sip of water from the glass next to her bed.

"I found no trace of any parents. In fact, I couldn't even find out where she'd been living, until I traced her phone number to a dumpy motel. Pretty creepy."

"Did you tell the police?" Lydia asked.

"Absolutely," he said. "They put the information in some file, but said there 'wasn't enough evidence to warrant an investigation.' She'd have to be reported as a missing person by an adult."

"I suppose everyone thinks I scared Paige away," Lydia said miserably.

Eric waved one hand in the air. "Who cares what they think? The only thing that matters is that I know the truth and your parents believe me."

"Parents?" Lydia asked.

"They, and Jake, have been here by your bedside every day since you got hurt. We all have."

"Mom and Dad—together?" This was almost as big a shock as her injury.

"Nice people. I've really gotten to know them both. And Jake's a totally cool kid."

"Yeah. He is." Lydia's eyes suddenly brimmed with tears. "I wish I'd spent more time with him."

Eric squeezed her hand. "Hey, you've been spending morning, noon, and night with him. You just didn't know it."

Lydia chuckled. There was so much to absorb. She felt like she'd been out of touch for three years, not three weeks.

"What about *Evita*?" she asked as the doctor and nurses gathered in the hall outside her room. "Did it open?"

"No, DYT temporarily postponed the show because of technical problems at the theater," Eric told her. "At least, that's the official version."

Lydia leaned back against her pillows, feeling

that people were so quick to think I was the bad one."

"Don't be so hard on yourself," Eric protested. "Remember, Paige was no slouch in getting people to believe—"

Lydia stopped him. "I didn't treat my friends very well. I always thought I should be the center of attention, and assumed that everyone agreed with me."

"What do you think now?" he asked.

She smiled wanly. "For starters, I think that my career at the Dallas Youth Theater is washed up."

"What are you going to do about it?"

"About DYT? Nothing," she said. "About my life—go on. Try to be kind to my friends and family. Maybe enjoy the world, what's left of this spring and the summer, instead of spending it cooped up in a dusty, dark theater."

"Enjoy the world . . . with me?" Eric asked with his boyish charm.

"Maybe," she replied with a flirtatious grin, the old spark back in her eyes. "And next year . . . I'm going to go to Juilliard, or the best theater school I can find!"

"That's the girl I love," Eric said softly.

"That's the girl I love," Eric said softly.

His words caught them both by surprise.

"Yes, love," he repeated. "Oh, sure, being a Leo, you can be unbearably ambitious, egocentric, boastful, insatiable in your need to be worshiped and adored, bored by puny details, reckless—"

"Oh, please," she interrupted. "Don't try to make me feel better!"

He smiled. "You're also trustworthy, responsible, a hard worker, talented, loving, adventuresome, and brave. *And*"—He raised a finger—"being a Leo, you're lucky to have strong recuperative powers. So I bet you'll fool all the doctors and be back on your feet in no time!"

"You really think so?" she asked.

He replied by brushing her cheek with a wonderful, princelike kiss. "I know so."

epilogue

The sun moves into your opposite sign,
Aquarius, and you are feeling very expan-
sive toward your friends. Be nice to them
on your way up—they will soften your
landing if you fall.

It was the final week in August, one week
before Lydia was to leave for New York and
drama school. It had been both an awful and
wonderful summer.

Awful, because Lydia's therapy to recover
from her injury had been slow and often painful.
It had only been in the past week or two, after
endless hours of stretching, weight training,
swimming, and deep massages, that she'd been
able to move without any physical reminders of
her injury.

Awful, because A. J., Robin, and the Caught
in the Act kids had ignored her totally.

Wonderful, because she had enjoyed planting
and tending a garden with her mom, and biking

with Jake. Wonderful, because her parents had really rallied around her recovery. Oh, there was no chance that they'd ever get back together, but at least there was some warmth between them for the first time since the divorce. Wonderful, because her hair had begun to grow back.

Wonderful, because she and Eric had become so close. He'd helped her with her physical therapy, pacing alongside her in the pool, taking long walks together, keeping her spirits high.

Although it hardly mattered to Lydia, *Evita* finally went up at DYT, with Jill playing the role that Lydia had once wanted so badly for herself. By all reports, Jill had done a credible, if far from spectacular job, although Lydia hadn't bothered to see the production. It cheered her when Eric reported overhearing audience members telling Bill Glover how much they missed seeing Lydia starring in a DYT show. And she smiled when Eric said that Keenan's voice had cracked during an important solo. She wasn't being mean-spirited; she was just putting DYT and that chapter of her life behind her.

Yes, she was definitely looking to the future, even though the thought of leaving her home and family—and Eric—and going off by herself to

New York frightened her on occasion. Still, she couldn't pass up the chance to pursue her dream of a life in the professional theater, and New York City was definitely the place to be.

For his part, Eric had been accepted to the University of Texas in Austin, but he planned to save his money and work hard at school. He hoped to transfer in his sophomore year to either New York University or the Pratt Institute in Brooklyn so he and Lydia could be together.

This particular afternoon, Lydia was alone in the house. Jake was off shooting hoops and her mother was at work, but that was okay. She was using the time alone to start the mammoth job of packing for her trip to New York. It was early afternoon, and she was expecting Eric to pick her up in a half hour to go the pool for their daily swim.

Ding-dong.

"That's funny." She glanced at the clock. "Eric's usually not this early."

Lydia was stunned to find A. J. and Robin standing on her porch when she opened the door.

Her first impulse was to slam the door in their faces, but they both looked so shamefaced that she waited to hear what they wanted.

"Lydia," A. J. began, "we know you must hate us, but we have something to show you."

"I don't hate you." Lydia pushed open the screen door and joined them on the porch.

"Do you want to tell her?" Robin asked A. J. "Or should I?"

"Tell me what?" Lydia asked. "What's wrong?" she added, suddenly alarmed.

A. J. sighed deeply. "Oh, Lydia . . ."

"What?" Lydia demanded. "What?"

Without another word, Robin thrust a newspaper clipping into Lydia's hand.

The clipping showed a photograph of a girl with a different hairstyle but most definitely Paige. Lydia read the accompanying article.

SUSPECT SOUGHT FOR ARSON MURDER

Police in Lawrence, Kansas, are seeking information about the whereabouts of the suspect wanted in connection with a fatal fire at a local theater. The fire, which occurred during a rehearsal of *Oklahoma!*, resulted in the death of a firefighter who arrived in response to the three-alarm call. The blaze, one of the worst in city history, was investigated by fire-department officials, who concluded it was arson.

The suspect, reportedly a seventeen-year-old actress new to the theater, is Sally Mae Jones, although police report this is an alias. Police have been unwilling to release details, but say the young woman has a history of mental problems, and warned the public to consider her dangerous.

"We called the Lawrence police," Robin said, his voice quaking. "We told them about Paige—or whatever her name really is. We told them about what happened to you."

"The police said they're very close to arresting her," A. J. added. "They need to piece together one or two final pieces of evidence first."

"But she won't get away?" Lydia asked.

"The police have her under round-the-clock surveillance. She won't get away," A. J. assured her.

"This is so horrible!" Robin kicked at the bits of gravel on Lydia's porch. "I can't believe how awful we treated you."

"Can you ever forgive us?" A. J. asked sincerely.

For an instant the hurt pride in Lydia wanted to say, "No." But she could see how genuinely upset and sorry her friends were. "Of course I forgive you," she said sadly. "Let's just put it behind us."

"You mean we're friends again?" A. J. asked, fighting back tears.

"We never stopped being friends," Lydia said, opening her arms to Robin and A. J.

The three friends, who had shared so much in their young lives, who were about to experience even more as they went their separate ways in life, embraced one another.

Eric had parked his van in the drive and was just coming up the walk when he saw them hugging.

"Now, that's just what I like to see," he said to Lydia, who smiled at him over A. J.'s shoulder. "A happy ending."

$1,000.00

FOR YOUR THOUGHTS

Let us know what you think. Just answer these seven questions and you could win $1,000! For completing and returning this survey, you'll be entered into a drawing to win a $1,000 prize.

OFFICIAL RULES: *No additional purchase necessary.* Complete the HarperPaperbacks questionnaire—be sure to include your name and address—and mail it, with first-class postage, to HarperPaperbacks, Survey Sweeps, 10 E. 53rd Street, New York, NY 10022. Entries must be received no later than midnight, October 4, 1995. One winner will be chosen at random from the completed readership surveys received by HarperPaperbacks. A random drawing will take place in the offices of HarperPaperbacks on or about October 16, 1995. The odds of winning are determined by the number of entries received. If you are the winner, you will be notified by certified mail how to collect the $1,000 and will be required to sign an affidavit of eligibility within 21 days of notification. A $1,000 money order will be given to the *sole winner* only—to be sent by registered mail. Payment of any taxes imposed on the prize winner will be the sole responsibility of the winner. All federal, state, and local laws apply. Void where prohibited by law. The prize is not transferable. **No photocopied entries.**

Entrants are responsible for mailing the completed readership survey to HarperPaperbacks, Survey Sweeps, at 10 E. 53rd Street, New York, NY 10022. If you wish to send a survey without entering the sweepstakes drawing, simply leave the name/address section blank. Surveys without name and address will not be entered in the sweepstakes drawing. HarperPaperbacks is not responsible for lost or misdirected mail. Photocopied submissions will be disqualified. Entrants must be at least 18 years of age and U.S. citizens. All information supplied is subject to verification. Employees, and their immediate family, of HarperCollins*Publishers* are not eligible. For winner information, send a stamped, self-addressed №10 envelope by November 10, 1995 to HarperPaperbacks, Sweeps Winners, 10 E. 53rd Street, New York, NY 10022.

Harper Paperbacks

would like to give you a chance to win $1,000.00
and all you have to do is answer these easy questions.
Please refer to the previous page for official rules and regulations.

Name: _____ Sex: M₀₁ F₀₂

Address: _____

City: _____ State: _____ Zip: _____

Age: 7-12₀₃   13-17₀₄   18-24₀₅   25-34₀₆   35-49₀₇   50+₀₈

We hope you enjoyed reading **Leo: Stage Fright**.

1 a) Did you intend to purchase this particular book?   Y₀₉ N₁₀
   b) Was this an impulse purchase?   Y₁₁ N₁₂

2) How important were the following in your purchase of this book?
(1 = not important; 3 = moderately important; 5 = very important)

word of mouth	1₁₃ 3₁₄ 5₁₅		advertising	1₃₁ 3₃₂ 5₃₃		
cover art & design	1₁₆ 3₁₇ 5₁₈		plot description	1₃₄ 3₃₅ 5₃₆		
cover glitz	1₁₉ 3₂₀ 5₂₁		price	1₃₇ 3₃₈ 5₃₉		
cover color	1₂₂ 3₂₃ 5₂₄		author	1₄₀ 3₄₁ 5₄₂		
floor stand/display	1₂₅ 3₂₆ 5₂₇		length of book	1₄₃ 3₄₄ 5₄₅		
contest offer	1₂₈ 3₂₉ 5₃₀					

3) In general, how do you find out about the books you want to read?

_____₄₆ word of mouth   _____₅₀ author publicity
_____₄₇ book reviews   _____₅₁ reader's clubs
_____₄₈ libraries   _____₅₂ advertising
_____₄₉ store browsing

4) Where did you buy this book?

Store Name: _____

City/State: _____

5) Have you ever listened to a book on tape?   Y₅₃   N₅₄

6) How many of the following do you buy each month?

mass market paperbacks	0₅₅	1-2₅₆	3-5₅₇	5+₅₈
large format paperbacks	0₅₉	1-2₆₀	3-5₆₁	5+₆₂
hardcovers	0₆₃	1-2₆₄	3-5₆₅	5+₆₆
spoken audio products/books on tape	0₆₇	1-2₆₈	3-5₆₉	5+₇₀

7) What types of books do you usually buy? (check all that apply)

_____₇₁ mystery/suspense/thriller   _____₇₇ romance/women's fiction
_____₇₂ science fiction/fantasy/horror _____₇₈ self-help/inspirational
_____₇₃ true crime   _____₇₉ entertainment/Hollywood
_____₇₄ westerns   _____₈₀ young adult (age 13+)
_____₇₅ reference   _____₈₁ children's (ages 7-12)
_____₇₆ business   _____₈₂ nonfiction/other

please return to:
HarperPaperbacks, Survey Sweeps, 10 East 53rd Street, New York, NY 10022